LOVING THE SCARRED SOLDIER

SECOND CHANCE REGENCY ROMANCE

ROSE PEARSON

LOVING THE SCARRED SOLDIER

PROLOGUE

Caldor House, Alnerton, 1807

"I will get you, Lady Charlotte Pierce," James whispered into her ear as he leaned just a smidge closer.

Charlotte looked over her shoulder to where Mrs. Crosby, her plump companion, was walking some feet behind them.

"Oh no you will not, James Watts, for I already have you," Charlotte replied cheekily, a playful grin on her face which exaggerated her dimples and the small cleft in her chin.

"Ah, but you only think that you have me. Truth be told, I have already laid claim to you these many years, but I allowed you to believe otherwise." He raised his chin slightly, the sun shining down on his handsome face. "There is no escaping it."

James folded his arms behind his back and Charlotte peered up at him. James and her brother William were the same age, but James was minutely taller, with broader shoulders and a more relaxed air about him. William, unfortunately, was often far too austere – a characteristic for which he could thank their father, the Duke of Mormont.

Charlotte kept watching James in silence, waiting until he turned back in her direction. The moment he did, she grinned at him and promptly stuck out her tongue.

"You always like to best me James, but I tell you, one day, I will be the one who claims victory. Not you."

He grinned, his bright smile illuminating his oval face and gently sloping cheekbones.

"I look forward to it. You could win me over for the rest of my life," he whispered.

Charlotte's heart fluttered in her chest.

"You should not say such things, James," she replied. "Someone might think you mean what you say."

Her fingers rose to coil a tress of dark brown hair. She wrapped it around her index finger several times as she kept her eyes to the ground, waiting for his reply.

"You know I always mean what I say," he answered tersely.

Charlotte's feet faltered with her heart. What was he saying? Lately, James's conversations were more and more personal, much more than they ever had been before. They'd long had a closeness between them, ever since her former governess, Mrs. Northam, had married his father, John, who acted as the Duchy of Mormont's solicitor. Now, however, things were changing.

Slowly, she looked up at him again and was met by the intensity of his emerald eyes. It made her heart gallop. She could not maintain the connection and quickly looked away.

"James, do not toy with me."

"I would never toy with you about such things," he replied calmly.

Again, Charlotte's eyes could not refrain from looking at him. In recent years she had often found herself admiring the man he had become. He was no longer the boy she'd run after and played games with all those years ago. He was a man of twenty, two years her elder, and more esteemed in her sight than any of their acquaintances, save her brother.

Charlotte stopped walking when she realized that James had failed to follow. She turned to face him, perplexity filling her heart. These feelings were strange to her. She had no mother to teach her, and with Mrs. Northam, now Mrs. Watts, no longer in her family employ, she was left to decipher the world on her own, for her nurse, Mrs. Crosby, was not someone whom she felt she could ask about important matters.

"Charlotte."

The sound of her name on his lips was a cherished utterance. She was very fond of it, more than she ever dared to admit. They knew each other too well - what she felt could not be what she thought it was. Could it? When he looked at her the way he was doing now, she believed that it could be.

"We have known each other for what seems a lifetime," James continued. The soft timbre of his voice was soothing. "We have played together and argued, cried, and laughed. We have seen each other in every... circumstance."

She laughed as the memory of their foray into his family's lakes, in nothing more than their undergarments as children suddenly flashed into her mind. Her father had been most upset by the indiscreet incident, which had left her soaked through, on the eve of a special dinner party. He had been equally displeased with the subsequent chill that had confined her to her bed. None of which had bothered her.

"We have."

James' brow furrowed slightly and she had the urge to smooth the wrinkles with her thumb. Customarily, she would have done so, but at that moment, with her feelings teetering on the brink, she dared not, lest they both fall over the edge.

Charlotte watched in curious fascination as the lump in James' throat bobbed up and down, and her dashing friend, ever confident, seemed to falter in his words. It was surprisingly endearing to see him so undone. She bit back a smile, but still felt the tug of it on her cheeks.

"You have to know... that is... you must be aware," James stuttered. His eyes were still lowered to his feet, but then, in a sudden burst of confidence, he forced himself to meet her gaze.

"Aware of what?" Charlotte questioned.

It took all of her strength to muster the words of the questions which curiosity demanded be answered. Did he feel as she did? Did his heart flutter at the sight of her as hers did whenever she saw him? Did he get cold, and his skin prickle when they touched? Was his head as full of her as hers was of him?

The more she thought of it, the more her emotions threatened to get the better of her. She quickly turned away, sure that her feelings were now evident on her face. She did not want to lose to him in this. She did not want to be the first to make her feelings known. In this one thing, she wanted to best him.

Charlotte's heart thundered in her ears. Her hands folded into defiant fists, as she determined not to be swayed by her emotions. She would be strong. She would let him speak and not give herself away, though she was aware that she may have already done so.

"Charlotte?" James' voice was a whisper. Then, she felt his hands settle gently on her arms. She was acutely aware of the proximity of his body to hers. This was not their normal interaction. Yes, they were close, had even embraced, but the feelings which filled her at that moment were far greater, more powerful – consuming. Her stomach felt as if it would take flight. "You feel it too, don't you?" he continued to whisper.

"Feel what?" Charlotte replied as her voice shook.

She glanced in the direction of Mrs. Crosby. The woman was pretending to look at the leaves on one of the potted plants, but glances in their direction made Charlotte aware that she was keeping a close eye on them, in case things went too far.

"She will not come. I asked her not to."

Charlotte's eyes widened and her breath caught in her throat at James' confession.

"You did what?"

"I asked Mrs. Crosby to give us a moment of privacy," he continued. "There is something very particular which I wish to say to you, Charlotte. Something best said to your face and not your back."

She could hear the slight lilt of laughter in his voice, but also nervousness.

"James," she replied. "You can tell me anything. You always have."

Her words were answered with a gentle tug on her arms, turning her to face him. She did not resist. She could not. All strength was gone from her limbs and she was at the mercy of her feelings, which would not be hidden.

Their eyes met and Charlotte thought she might faint. Her head felt light, her heart was gone, only large butterfly wings remained, beating frantically in her chest, as smaller ones filled her belly. What was happening?

He did not remove his hands from her arms, Instead, he stepped closer, and Charlotte felt sure that the world had stopped and she no longer remembered how to breathe.

"You and William have always been my dearest friends," James stated. "But you, Charlotte, you have become something infinitely more dear to me." Warmth washed up her neck and she was sure that her cheeks were now painted in crimson. Yet she could not speak. "I know that you have only ever considered me as a friend, and for a long time, I had accepted that fact. I thought I could live with it, but I cannot. I cannot be content with simply being your friend when I desire to be something much more."

Charlotte raised a hand and placed it on his chest to stop him, but the beating beneath her fingers caused her to pause. His heart was racing just like hers.

James looked at her delicate fingers and then placed his hand over hers, holding it over his heart.

"This is what I feel every time I am near you. I cannot stop it. I have tried, but nothing works. I think it is because I do not wish it to. I like that you do this to me. You are the only one who can."

Her breathing erratic, Charlotte tried to think. She knew all the proper things to do, the decorum that was required, but how did one have such decorum with someone who had nursed your wounds and wiped your tears, often after having been responsible for causing them? One who knew you better than anyone else did?

"I know there are many who desire you," James continued. "I am not so foolish as to believe that I am the only one who cares for you, but I would hope I might have some advantage over those others."

"Of whom do you speak? I know of no one," Charlotte questioned, bewildered.

His emerald eyes were ablaze.

"Do you mean to tell me that there is no other who wishes your hand?"

Charlotte's hearing became hollow, only the sound of what seemed to be rushing water could be heard as the words left his lips. She was eighteen. She had never had anyone desire her hand, at least not that she knew of.

Such matters were for her father, and none dared speak to her before presenting their proposal to him. None but James, that is. He was allowed certain liberties that other gentlemen were not, being such a close family friend.

"What are you saying?" she whispered, "Be plain."

He smiled at her.

"Always so straightforward."

"Always skirting around the subject," she replied. "Just tell me. Do not keep me on tenterhooks." She squeezed his hand lightly. "I want to hear the words."

James stepped closer, the space between them almost entirely gone as he lowered his head to her ear and whispered.

"I love you, Charlotte. I have always loved you."

The smile his words elicited could not be contained, and as their eyes met, she answered him.

"I love you, too, James. I always have."

～

CALDOR HOUSE, Alnerton, 1809

"LADY CHARLOTTE. LADY CHARLOTTE." A soft voice repeated her name, but Charlotte was doing her utmost to resist. "You must rouse yourself, Lady Charlotte. The day is already upon us and you must get ready."

It was Sophie Lefebvre, her new companion. Her father had finally been swayed to Charlotte's view that Mrs. Crosby was no longer suitable and that a woman closer to her age would be a far better choice. Sophie, who was also almost twenty, the daughter of an English-woman and a Frenchman, her family in exile from France as a result of the war, had seemed a good choice to replace Mrs. Crosby.

Charlotte forced her dark brown eyes open. The room was still mostly in darkness, but Sophie had the chambermaids already at work opening the blinds, while she set about laying out Charlotte's attire in readiness.

"Please, Lady Charlotte. You do not want to keep your brother and the duke waiting. It would be disre-spectful to Monsieur Watts if you were to arrive late," Sophie pleaded. "You would not want to do that."

Sophie knew those words would force Charlotte from her bed, though no words could change how Charlotte felt, not on that day.

Charlotte forced herself to rise from her four-poster bed, then padded to the window, her bare feet making no noise as she crossed the room. She looked out to where grey mists covered the gardens. The sky was overcast and the sun was completely hidden. It was as if the day shared her feelings.

"Quickly, Lady Charlotte," Sophie continued. She came to stand beside Charlotte. "I know that you do not wish to go, but you must."

"Must I?" Charlotte retorted weakly. "It will change nothing."

Sophie sighed.

"No, it will not. It is not supposed to. It is for you to show the respect which Monsieur Watts deserves. Please, come from the window and let me help you dress."

Charlotte was a doll in Sophie's hands. She turned

her and twisted her, made her sit, and stand, all while Charlotte uttered not a word. Finally, once her shoes were on and her black dress laced and every adornment in place, she sat her before the mirror.

The young woman who looked back at her was foreign to her eyes. Her skin was far paler than it used to be. Her eyes less bright and her long dark brown hair seemed a dull greyish-black. Everything seemed to be cast in shades of grey.

The white collar which rose around her neck itched, but Charlotte cared little about it. It was the only contrast to the black of the rest of her ensemble. Once her hair was curled and pinned, Sophie placed a black feathered cap on her head.

"C'est fini! You are done!"

Charlotte didn't reply. Instead, she stood and strode out of her chamber.

She found William loitering in the hall, waiting for her. Her brother was not himself either, as was evident from the solemn expression on his face. He walked toward her and took her hand, hooking it gently over his arm.

"How are you this morning, Charlotte? We missed you at breakfast."

"How should I be?" she answered absently.

Her eyes glanced over the balcony to the floor below.

"It was a foolish question," William replied. "Forgive me. I do not know how to deal with these matters."

She turned to her brother.

"Save Mother, we are unaccustomed to such things. You are forgiven."

He smiled at her before proceeding, in silence, to escort her down the stairs and out the door, to where the carriage waited for them. It was decorated appropriately; pulled by matched black horses with black plumes upon their heads. The driver was similarly dressed in black and the carriage was of the same color.

Charlotte's feet faltered, but William bore her up and helped her inside. Their father was already waiting.

"That took you too long," he commented harshly. "It isn't right to be late for such things. It is gross disrespect, Charlotte. You should know better. Both of you."

"Forgive me, Father," William replied. "It was my fault entirely."

"All the worse. You, being the elder, should direct your sister appropriately, and not pander to such poor conduct. See to it that it never happens again."

"Of course, Father. Never again," William replied.

Charlotte remained silent, and as the carriage moved forward, her gaze stayed fixed out the window.

She recognized none of the landscape as they passed, her mind too full to allow her to truly see what was before her, and she shunned the sight of Watton Hall, James' former home. She could not look upon it without losing her composure. She chose to close her eyes until she was sure they were well past it. The next sight she saw, consequently, was that of Alnerton Village Church.

The chapel was overflowing with mourners, but a special place had been reserved for them, and William helped her to it. Charlotte sat in silence, refusing to look at the empty coffin at the front of the church.

James was not there. His body had been lost somewhere in Roliça, Portugal, where he'd fallen during the battle with the French the year before. It had taken months for them to get news of his death, and more still for his father to come to terms with it, enough to have the memorial service held.

They all struggled to believe it – Captain James Watts, a fine young man, his father's pride and joy, an adoring stepson and caring and devoted friend, and the man Charlotte loved, was dead.

The Reverend Moore said a great many things about James, but they were only shadows of the truth. James was far more than the vicar claimed. The vicar hadn't known James as she did.

She could have told them of the man he truly was, the gentle soul who'd tended her knee when she fell among the brambles. The man who'd taken every opportunity to touch her hand whenever he could, and who had loved to make her laugh.

The man whose face she still saw every time she closed her eyes.

Once the rites were performed, Charlotte and her family gathered with Mr and Mrs Watts to bury the son they'd lost.

She was coping, in control, until the moment the pallbearers brought the coffin to the grave. Then, Charlotte lost all semblance of calm.

The tears flowed from her eyes and her body was wracked with uncontrollable spasms. She gasped for breath but found none. She was suffocating where she stood. The air she struggled to breathe was gone. James was gone.

William did his best to console her, but there was no consolation for her grief - it was a physical pain she could not bear, and she crumbled under the weight of it. Seconds later, her brother's strong arms were carrying her away from the sight, away from sympathetic, pitying eyes, to the safety of their carriage. Their father followed close behind, and soon they were on their way home.

Charlotte had no recollection of the return journey. Her room was dark when she awoke, much later, and she was still dressed in her mourning gown. Her feathered cap was gone.

She rolled onto her back but no sooner had she done so than fresh tears rolled down her cheeks. He was gone. James was never coming back.

It was heartbreak like no other. She had been a child, barely two, when her mother had passed away, and she had no true recollection of that loss. James, though, was different. She had known him. She had cared for him. She had loved him.

Silent tears kept her company as she lay in the dark until her eyes could weep no more. Then, Charlotte forced herself to sit up. The gloom of her room was oppressive - she needed to escape it, she needed light to help her fight the darkness which threatened to overtake her. She rushed to her chamber door, forgetting to don stockings or shoes, and simply walked along the corridor with no plan of where she was going.

Soon, she heard her father's voice. She followed it until she stood outside his office. She listened; he was in conversation with someone - her brother William she was sure - and she heard her name mentioned.

"The Marquess of Dornthorpe?" her brother asked.

"Yes. He has written to propose his interest in an alliance between our families. He is seeking your sister's hand for his son, Malcolm, Earl of Benton."

"Father, it is too soon to present such a proposal to Charlotte. She is still mourning for James."

"She will recover. Such an alliance should be most agreeable to all parties. However, I note your point. I will give her a few weeks to mourn his loss before informing her of the betrothal."

"Betrothal? Father, don't you think it prudent to ask Charlotte if she has any interest in the man before arranging an engagement. She has met him but four times, if I remember right. And a betrothal during mourning – that will set the gossips' tongues wagging."

"Four times was more than enough for your mother to decide to marry me. I do not see why your sister should be any different. As for the gossips – well, technically, James is no relation of ours, and so mourning is not a requirement."

"Father, please..."

"I have made my decision, William. Your sister will marry Malcolm Tate, and become the Countess of Benton, and eventually the Marchioness of Dornthorpe. Our family will sit on two seats, Dornthorpe and Mormont. Such a fortunate alliance is to be envied indeed."

Her knees gave out and the floor rushed up, as Charlotte slumped against the wall. That was it? James was barely in his grave and yet she was given to another? It was at that moment that she realized how conniving her father truly was. He cared nothing for her pain and hurt, only for their family's good standing.

Charlotte had no strength to remove herself from outside the door. *Let them find me here*, she thought. *Let them know that I am aware of what they had discussed without her. Let them see what it has done to me. Maybe that would touch father's heart.*

She might hope so, but she suspected it was unlikely.

CHAPTER ONE

Caldor House, Alnerton, 1814

C harlotte looked up at the imposing building toward which they were driving. Caldor House was still the same, all these years later, and as it had in the past, it filled her heart with heaviness. The only reason she was returning to her father's home was for the sake of her son. George needed a male influence, and without his father, he had only her father and William to guide him, for her late husband's father now had suffered a debilitating illness.

She looked over to where her sleeping child lay. He was so much like Malcolm that it made her smile to think of it. She stroked his hair gently. She had not loved Malcolm when she'd married him, but he was the escape she'd needed – from grief and from loneliness.

In return, she had given him the gift of their son – the

son he had hoped for, to carry on his family name. She was happy that she'd been able to do so before his time on earth was over. Her only regret was that he would not be there to see George grow into a man he would be proud of.

The carriage stopped on the broad expanse of gravel in front of the house. The door opened, and there, standing in his usual fine attire, was her brother William. A broad smile spread across his face as he immediately took the stairs at a rapid pace to come toward her.

"Charlotte!" he called.

She smiled in return as the coachman opened the door for her and helped her down.

"William, how wonderful to see you."

She wrapped her arms around him. It felt like a lifetime since they had last seen each other, and she had missed him dearly - it was his presence here, more than anything, which had brought her back to her childhood home.

"How was your journey?" William asked.

"Long and tiring. George is asleep in the carriage," Charlotte replied.

"Then I shall gather him up and carry him into the house."

William strode toward the carriage and, moments later, cradled her son in his arms. George looked angelic, nestled against his uncle's chest, completely safe from all harm.

It wasn't easy being alone and so far from home. Once Malcolm had died, everything had changed. Suddenly the security Charlotte knew no longer existed.

There was also the threat from those who wished to take from her son what was rightfully his, the title of Earl of Benton, and, likely quite soon, that of Marquess of Dornthorpe, when his ailing grandfather died. He was too young, but he would learn under her father, and when he was old enough, he would return and take his place. In the meantime, Malcolm's trusted steward, Mr. Charlesworth, was tending to matters and would send Charlotte regular reports.

"He weighs nothing," William commented as they walked up the stairs.

"To you perhaps, but to me, he weighs little less than a ton," Charlotte mused. "Is Father at home?"

William's expression fell.

"He had to remain in town to see to some pressing matters with our bankers. I have only just returned myself. I wanted to be here for your arrival. Father will return by tea time."

Charlotte nodded in understanding - it was for the best that her father was not present. It gave her time to settle herself, to some extent, before seeing him again. Since her marriage, Charlotte had seen little of her father. He had stayed in Alnerton or at their townhouse in London and found no reason to visit her, not even at the birth of his grandson, although he had sent a card and an expensive gift.

"I have prepared your old rooms for you and converted the adjoining suite into a nursery for George. I thought it best to keep him near you. He will be unfamiliar with these surroundings for a time."

Charlotte smiled.

"Thank you, William. You think of everything."

"I try to," he replied with a grin. "Especially when it comes to matters of my sister and nephew."

They were greeted at the door by almost all of the household staff, their smiling faces bright as they welcomed her back. Charlotte was slightly overwhelmed. She'd almost forgotten them, for she had put Caldor House behind her on the day she'd left, thinking she would never return to it. Unfortunately, fate had other plans for her, and here she was.

Once the welcome was over, she followed William upstairs as footmen scurried to unload all of her possessions and carry the steamer trunks up to her rooms. William carried George into the nursery and settled him into bed without him even waking. Leaving a nursemaid watching over him as he slept, William opened the door and ushered her through into her rooms.

The space was bright, the curtains pulled wide to allow the sun into the room, but the memories lingered there. She could remember the last night she'd spent in that room, and the many before that, filled with hopes, fears, and then abiding grief.

I thought never to see this room again, yet, here I am.

"Is everything to your liking?" William said from behind her.

Charlotte turned to him, slowly untying the ribbon from beneath her chin as she removed her bonnet.

"Everything is just as I remember it."

"I wanted it to be as easy an adjustment for you as possible."

He smiled at her.

"I missed you very much," Charlotte replied.

Sadness began to prick her eyes with tears.

"And I, you," William replied as she strode toward him.

She fell into her brother's embrace and held him tightly as memories overwhelmed her. His hand gently patted her back as he spoke soothingly in her ear.

"I know it has been frightfully difficult for you, Charlotte. I wish I could have made it better. A thousand times I have wished I could have changed the things that happened, but I hope you know I had no control over those circumstances."

"Hush," Charlotte urged. "Do not speak of it. I know what you would have done if you could." She looked up at him. "Now, leave me alone for a while. I shall rest before tea."

"Of course."

William nodded and excused himself.

She lay back on the bed intending to rest, but her mind resisted that intent. Memories tumbled through her mind, leaving her wide awake and out of sorts. She lay on her bed, her hands clasped over her stomach as she looked up at the canopy above her, until the exhaustion from the long day of travel, and all that had gone before, caught up with her, and sleep overtook her.

It was nearly teatime when Charlotte awoke. Immediately, she worried about George, but when she called for the maid, she was assured that George had eaten his meal, had looked in to see his mother sleeping, and had happily gone back into the nursery with the maid, to play with his toys.

Charlotte allowed the maid to dress her in a gown suitable for dining with her father. Her father kept an elegant table at all times and expected everyone to conform to his expectations.

Her dress was mint green in color, made from the finest silk and lace. It had been a gift from Malcolm before he became ill. Charlotte was glad that, now her mourning was done, she could wear colors again. The year of mourning had taken a toll on her, shut away at Bentonmere Park, but it had also been peaceful. Now, for George's sake, it was time to be visible to the world again.

She smoothed her hands over her stomach as she looked at her reflection in the mirror. Her shape had changed after having George. She no longer had a girl's figure, but it was a pleasing figure nonetheless. She twisted a curl of dark hair around her finger then pushed it back into place before turning away.

The dining room was set when Charlotte arrived. William lingered by the door waiting for her.

"Father isn't here as yet," he informed her.

"Shall we sit then and wait?"

"We may as well. You know how he is about punctuality, even if he is not so himself," her brother answered with a light laugh.

He hooked his arm and held it out to her.

Charlotte allowed her brother his little trifles of amusement. He'd had so little of humor in his youth, for he'd lived under their father's thumb, ever aware that he was to inherit his title and position, as Duke, and also his vast portfolio of investments, in banking and shipping. It had always been a heavy burden for William to bear, and because of that, Charlotte hardly ever allowed herself the luxury of sharing her burdens with her brother.

James had always been the person she'd shared such things with.

The thought of her former love gave her a moment of pause. It always did. Despite his death, James Watts had really never left her, even throughout her marriage, he was, in a way, ever-present. He was still a comfort to her in her thoughts, even if he was no longer in the world.

"How are Father's affairs?" she questioned once they were seated.

William sighed.

"When it comes to matters pertaining to the smooth running of the Duchy, it is never a straightforward task. Father insists upon seeing to every detail, no matter how small. He leaves me little responsibility – though he expects me to pay as close attention as he does himself."

She looked at him with concern. He was clearly frustrated at the lack of trust their father was showing him.

"Do you like it at all? Working with Father, I mean?"

"There are days when I love it. Learning about all the elements involved in the Duchy's management, from managing the rents to investing the proceeds from the land well – it is absorbing and challenging. Many in Father's place would entrust such work to managers and bailiffs – but he prides himself that it is a matter of honor."

"Has there been some cause for a loss?"

Charlotte shook her head lightly. Her brother was a clever man. He had left Cambridge with high praise from his tutors, and he was not one to shirk his duties. But

Father was very demanding. It could only be hard on William to have to always listen and never be permitted to give his opinion or have any autonomy.

They were sipping wine and talking when their father finally arrived. He marched into the room without care or apology and promptly seated himself at the head of the table.

"Charlotte," he stated. "I am glad to see that you that have arrived and remembered how I prefer to go on here."

"Thank you, Father."

"Where is the boy?"

"George is with Mrs. White, his nurse. He will be in bed by now."

"Good, a boy needs routine and order - structure makes a man," her father continued. He picked up the small bell which sat to his right and rang it, as an indication to the staff to serve dinner.

The meal was delicious - four courses as usual - including dessert. Her father always insisted upon it, although why she never knew. It was simply the way it was.

"How is Mrs. Watts, William? Has she improved at all?" her father asked through a mouthful of the roast.

"I'm afraid not, Father. Mr Watts told me only yesterday that she has taken a turn for the worse."

"Unfortunate. We are sure to have a funeral to attend soon," her father continued.

Charlotte dropped her knife in alarm.

"Funeral? Is Mrs. Watts so ill?"

"I am afraid so," William explained. "It has been

several months now since she first became ill and there seems to be no end in sight. I am sorry to have to tell you this on your first day back."

She could hardly think. Beatrice Watts was the only mother figure Charlotte had ever known. The thought of her death was unbearable. How would her husband take that news after already having lost James?

"I will go to see her tomorrow," Charlotte blurted.

It was her father's turn to drop his cutlery. However, he recovered quickly and carried on as if nothing had happened.

"I do not think that is wise, Charlotte. Mrs. Watts is very ill and you have a child to consider. You cannot allow yourself to be so exposed."

"What exposure can there be, Father? I will take the customary precautions. I am sure that you and William have visited her, and neither of you has become ill."

"I think Father is correct, Charlotte. You have only just returned here, perhaps you should allow yourself some time to adjust before visiting the Watts," William agreed.

She looked at him perplexed.

"William, Mrs. Watts has tended to us our entire lives. How can I be so unfair as to avoid her, especially under these circumstances? I cannot. I will not. I shall visit her tomorrow."

The subject died immediately, but Charlotte did not miss the silent exchange between her brother and father, an exchange of looks which puzzled her completely. She did not understand their thinking but she would not be persuaded by it. Mrs. Watts was a lovely woman and she would see her, and care for her if it would give her any comfort at all.

After tea, Charlotte retreated to the parlor, but she was not alone for long. Mrs. White brought George to her soon after, the young child having woken fretful and calling for her. She set her son on the floor with his blocks and joined him.

"A little of this and you will be tired again in no time, won't you George?" she said as she placed one block on top of the other. George hit the floor with his.

They continued like that for several minutes before they were joined by William. Her brother watched them with a silent grin as they played. His presence was comforting and Charlotte was happy to have him there and thankful that their father was absent.

"I am sorry I could not stay long after the funeral," William said suddenly.

Charlotte looked at him perplexed.

"Why do you bring it up?"

"I do not think I have apologized enough for it. You needed me after his passing and I could not be there for you as I should."

"William, you had pressing work. I understood," Charlotte assured him.

William had only stayed a fortnight after Malcolm was laid to rest. Charlotte had wanted him to stay longer, but the management of the estates and the investments had called him away, and she could not bring herself to ask him to prolong his stay regardless. She held no grudge toward him for it. It was the way of the world, and her loss was no large factor in his life, only hers.

"Thank you, Charlotte. You have always been too kind in everything," William continued. "Do you still intend to visit Mrs. Watts tomorrow?"

"Of course," she replied. "I said I would and I shall do so. I shall make arrangements in the morning to visit her during the afternoon."

William was silent for a moment. Charlotte could see he was contemplating something, more than likely the bank, or next year's crop plantings on one of the estates – he never stopped thinking of such things, it seemed to her.

"Will you excuse me, Charlotte? I have a matter I must urgently attend to."

"Of course."

William came to them and ruffled George's hair before leaving the room. Charlotte remained with her son, playing with his blocks until his eyes grew heavy again, and he curled beside her on the floor to sleep.

She lifted George and carried him from the room, leaving the blocks where they lay, holding his head gently against her shoulder as she walked toward the stairs and their rooms. On her way up, she happened to turn, and glance down, to see William giving a letter to a footman, who immediately left the house. Her brow furrowed. Who was William writing to at such an hour?

CHAPTER TWO

Watton Hall, Alnerton

"It is wonderful to see you again, Charlotte."

Beatrice Watts' voice was a raspy shadow of its former sweetness. Charlotte longed to hear that sweetness return.

She stroked the older woman's greying hair, and the memory of its former lustrous brown remained clear in her mind. Charlotte had often envied those beautiful tresses, but now they were thin and dry, all of the shine gone.

"How could I stay away when you are ill?"

Mrs. Watts smiled.

"You are such a lovely, considerate girl. You always were."

Charlotte giggled.

"What is it?" Mrs. Watts questioned.

"You called me a girl," Charlotte answered. "I have not been called that in years," she mused. "It was quite refreshing to hear."

"You will always be a girl to me," Mrs. Watts replied. Her words were broken by a harsh cough that shook her entire body.

Charlotte looked at her with concern. She was so frail, and the cough seemed to want to divide her bones from her flesh, it was so violent. It took Mrs. Watts several minutes to recover.

"I'm sorry, dear," she said. "This cough just seems to get worse and worse."

Charlotte patted her hand.

"There is no need to apologize."

"I am surprised your father allowed you to visit," Mrs. Watts continued. "I know his feelings about contracting ailments. I did not think he would want you here."

"Father tried to dissuade me, but I insisted on coming. Even William did not want me to, but I refused to be denied." She smiled at the older woman. "I simply had to see you. I had to know how you were for myself."

"I am thankful that you came," Mrs. Watts replied. She squeezed Charlotte's hand but the action was barely felt; it was so weak. Charlotte worried more.

"I am happy I could be here," Charlotte replied. "I could not stay away. I wanted just to see you, but I realized the truth was, I was afraid."

"Afraid?"

"Yes, afraid," Charlotte replied. "When I heard of your illness and how severe it was, I worried I might not see you again, ever. My dear Mrs. Watts, the thought of losing you is an unbearable one. I had no choice but to come today, even if only to assuage my fears. You have been there my entire life. Every good memory I have includes you. I cannot imagine a world without you."

The two women sat smiling together for some time, and Charlotte held Mrs. Watts' hand as she began to cough relentlessly.

"How long have you had this?" Charlotte questioned once Mrs. Watts caught her breath.

"Many months now," she replied. "It started as hardly anything, a trifle, but then it just got worse and worse. Do not trouble yourself with my ailment. It is not every day that you return to this county. I want to hear everything about life outside of Alnerton. What was it like being married?"

Charlotte thought about her marriage to Malcolm – it had been a wonderful one, the best she could imagine it to be, yet it had still lacked something.

"It was wonderful," she replied "Malcolm was a good man, kind and considerate in everything, and he treated me like a queen. He so loved our son, George. It is my only regret that he could not live to see him grow up." It was a weight that hung upon her heavily. The future of her son lay in her hands. It was that, and his need for male supervision and direction, which steered the course of their lives now. "However, I will do my best to raise him as Malcolm would have wanted. Malcolm had such wonderful ambitions for his son, the next Marquess of Dornthorpe." Charlotte's eyes lowered and her head hung low. "But may I confess something?" she said softly.

Mrs. Watts' brow furled lightly.

"What do you need to confess?"

"I was happy with Malcolm," she admitted. "However, I believe that, though he made me very happy, I should have been happier with James."

Charlotte's brown eyes rose to meet Mrs. Watts' blue ones. The older woman looked at her with a tender smile.

"You still remember James, my dear?"

"Oh yes. I have never forgotten him," Charlotte answered. A small smile tugged at the corners of her lips as she remembered the man whose love had held her heart all of these years. "How do you forget one who lives inside you?"

Mrs. Watts' eyes lowered sadly and she patted Charlotte's knuckles.

"I suppose I thought you would forget him after all this time. I warrant I should have known better. You and James shared such love for ones so young."

"I often felt guilty," Charlotte admitted. "Malcolm gave me such a wonderful life, and I should have been happier, but I was never whole. Part of me died when James did, and there was no resurrecting it." Once again, Mrs. Watts attempt to squeeze her hand, and again, the pressure was negligible. Charlotte was thankful, all the same, for the small comfort she attempted to give, even in her frail condition. "You understand, don't you? It was not that I was unhappy about the marriage. I needed it. I was lost after James died and with my father being as he is, Malcolm was my only means of escape, so I jumped at it. And truly, I do not regret the choice. It gave me George and some very happy memories."

"What did your husband die from?" Mrs. Watts asked. "I never heard."

"They say it was pneumonia. It came upon him suddenly and took him quickly. I nursed him as best I could, right to the end. I was thankful I could be there with him." Once again Charlotte's eyes lowered. "But, to my shame, it made me think of James. There was no one with him in the end. No one to comfort him in his pain and tell him he was loved and that it was all right to move on. I've often thought of that over the years. How horrible it must've been for him to die in that way. I suppose it was why I insisted on being there with Malcolm at the end."

"You were an excellent wife, Charlotte. Never doubt that." Mrs. Watts stated.

Charlotte was incredulous at the woman's intuitiveness.

"How can you say that? How can you know what I did, and what my doubts are?"

"I know you, my child. Your feelings are often good but laced with guilt when they conflict with other feelings," Mrs. Watts said with a smile. "If there is a flaw in you, that would be the one."

Charlotte laughed heartily.

"I assure you I have flaws enough, Mrs. Watts."

The older woman laughed too, although it was a soft sound that ended in a cough.

"Not that I have ever seen. In my eyes, you will always be the most pleasant, compassionate, and understanding child I ever had the pleasure to raise. You and William were the pinnacles of my life. If I had children of my own, I would wish them to be just like you. Although, I would also wish that William had a father who was easier on him."

Charlotte nodded in silent agreement. Her brother, for all his goodness, lacked one thing: love. It was the one thing he wanted from their father and the one thing he was always denied. William was never good enough in their father's eyes, and he constantly sought to improve him, which only served to make William doubt himself most of the time. This situation had improved over the years but it was something she knew her brother still struggled with and it weighed upon him.

"Is it almost dinner?" Mrs. Watts asked.

Her eyes were hooded and Charlotte could see that she was fatigued. Charlotte checked the clock on the mantel.

"Very nearly, Mrs. Watts. Are you very hungry?"

Mrs. Watts nodded.

"Then I shall see to it that your dinner is brought up immediately."

Charlotte left Mrs. Watts to rest while she made her way below stairs to find the Watts' cook. The house was silent as she walked along the hall that led to the stairs. It was lined by half a dozen doors, each leading to a separate room. This wing had once been Mr. Watts' mother's accommodation until her passing many years ago. Suddenly, a door creaked behind her. Charlotte turned abruptly to find the source of the sound but saw nothing.

"Is someone there?" She waited, listening carefully, but there was no answer. She called again and still, there was no reply. "That was odd," she said to herself as she moved on.

Charlotte found the housekeeper, Mrs. Boyle, going about her duties and asked when dinner would be served. She returned to Mrs. Watts with that information, and Mrs. Watts promptly invited her to stay and dine with her husband.

"It would delight him to see you. He has missed you as much as I have," Mrs. Watts assured her.

Charlotte rubbed the older woman's hand gently.

"Then I will send word to father that I shall dine here tonight."

"Wonderful!"

Mrs. Watts's constitution could not cope with a vigorous meal, and so her supper consisted of warm broth and some rustic bread. Charlotte stayed to feed it to her, as her former governess seemed unable to do so herself. Mrs. Watts was in a sorry state indeed.

Charlotte took the tray back downstairs and was delighted to come across Mr Watts in the hallway.

"Lady Charlotte," John Watts bowed to her politely "Umm, sorry, Lady Benton – in my mind you are always the little girl I knew."

"Mr. Watts!"

Charlotte bobbed a curtsey respectfully.

"I heard of your return from your father," Mr Watts said. "But I did not expect to see you here this evening. This is a very pleasant surprise."

John Watts was a man with a kindly nature. He was a serious man of the law and of business, but he had more cause for smiles and mirth than many at home. Raised as the only son of a country cleric, his good fortunes in life ensured his good temperament.

"What is this?" he asked, taking note of the supper tray in Charlotte's hands

"I have just come from giving Mrs. Watts her dinner," Charlotte explained. "I was returning the tray to the kitchen."

"Not a bit of that," Mr. Watts replied cheerfully, and promptly took the tray from her hand and set it on the sideboard nearby. "You will not be returning trays when you are here, and just come back to the country. You must tell me everything that has happened while you were gone."

Charlotte smiled as he hooked her arm over his and began to walk in the direction of the parlor.

"How was your journey? Was the weather favorable? How was life at Bentonmere Park? Is your son with you?"

The quick succession of his questions made Charlotte giggle.

"I will tell you everything over dinner," she replied. "Mrs. Watts has invited me to dine with you this evening and I have accepted."

"She is a perceptive woman. Quite forward-thinking," Mr. Watts commented. "I am happy she took the initiative, for I would have done the same myself. You have been sorely missed in these parts. I, for one, have missed your visits and your cheerfulness."

"I have missed you too, Mr. Watts," Charlotte replied with a smile.

He smiled back at her.

"I must freshen up before dinner. Would you wait for me in the parlor?"

"That would be no trouble. I have to send a note to my father, letting him know that I will be staying here for dinner tonight."

"I shall find my footman, Porter, He will deliver the message for you." Mr. Watts released her hand. "I will see to it myself, and you see to your note. I will look in on Beatrice before I return. Shall we meet in the dining room in fifteen minutes?"

Charlotte nodded.

"Capital! Here is Porter now." He turned his attention to the footman, "Lady Benton has a note to send. Will you see to it?"

"Have you the note ready?" Porter asked.

"No, I have not," Charlotte replied. "I will need pen, ink, and paper."

"You can find some in the small escritoire in the parlor," said Mr Watts. "We always keep some on hand down here. In the meantime, I will leave you to it."

Charlotte found the writing implements and dropped into the chair at the escritoire to write the note to her father. She had just completed it when she noticed another note half-tucked beneath the tray which sat on one end of the small desk. Her brow furrowed at the sight, as the handwriting on that note looked remarkably like William's. However, she did not think about it long, being more focused on finding Porter and sending the note off to her father. Then as instructed, she waited for Mr. Watts in the dining room.

They had a delightful meal, full of good food and

even better conversation. Mr. Watts was nothing like her father. He spoke openly and laughed heartily, allowing her to speak as much as he did. Her father, by comparison, held a monopoly on the conversation at every opportunity.

"Do you remember that incident with you, James, William, and the bees?" Mr. Watts asked with a laugh. "We must've heard you screaming for a mile as you charged towards the house."

"How could I forget? It was the most frightening experience of my life!" Charlotte replied with a laugh.

"James came home with so many stings I thought he would surely swell to ten times his size," Mr. Watts replied.

"I am sure you were much better about it than my father. He forbade William and me from visiting you for over a week. Not that it stopped us from doing the very same thing a week later," she mused with a smile.

The grandfather clock in the room chimed, alerting them to the fact that the hour was now nine. Charlotte looked at it with disappointment.

"How quickly the time passes," she commented. "I'm afraid it is time for me to leave you. My father and William will be expecting me and they are of the sort who will not sleep until I return, although George will have grumbled, then fallen asleep regardless," Charlotte said with some amusement.

"Then we shall not keep you."

Mr. Watts rose from his seat to pull out hers. Once again, he hooked her arm through his as he escorted her from the room.

"It has been most pleasant to have you here this evening, my dear," he stated as they strolled from the room. "I am sure your presence has done more good for Beatrice's health than any doctor's medicine ever could. You have a way of lightening the room and lifting the spirits whenever you're in it. I have had the benefit of your bonhomie this evening. I hope it will not be too long before I have the pleasure of it again."

Charlotte smiled. "Wild horses could not keep me away."

Mr. Watts led her to the stairs and up to say goodbye to Mrs. Watts. On the way, Charlotte once again heard the same strange noise and felt as if she was being watched.

"Did you hear that?" she asked.

"Hear what? I did not hear anything," Mr. Watts replied.

Charlotte frowned slightly. "Just now I thought I heard a door creak as if someone had opened it. Did you hear nothing?"

Mr. Watts shook his head. "Nothing. Perhaps it was something from below stairs?"

"Perhaps," Charlotte replied, though she was not sure if it.

Mr. Watts patted her hand gently. "Watton Hall is an old house. Many things creak."

Charlotte smiled and nodded. "A good point, Mr. Watts. I should say goodbye to Mrs. Watts."

The pair proceeded to Mrs Watts' bedchamber and the strange happening was quickly forgotten.

CHAPTER THREE

A veil of darkness cloaked him from view as he looked down at Charlotte's departing form. He watched her in silence, the anxiety and thrill of seeing her held at bay by his desire to remain concealed.

James placed a hand upon the frame of the window and braced himself as the weight of his emotions bore down on him.

When he'd received William's note the night before, telling of Charlotte's pending visit, James had immediately decided that he would do everything in his power to avoid seeing her. It made no sense to do so. Charlotte still believed the lie that had been told for so many years. The lie of his death on the battlefield. The truth was far worse, in his opinion, and he would protect her from it.

Yet, when the time came, and she was once again beneath his family's roof, he found he could not keep his word even to himself.

Charlotte, as he had expected, was radiant. The moment that James saw her dark hair emerge from the confines of her carriage, he knew he could not stay away. He'd hidden behind the tapestry which covered the entry to the adjoining room to his stepmother's bedchamber. He could be close enough to hear her laughter, and yet remain invisible.

He'd watched her, considering every contour of her delicate features, remembering the way she used to smile at him and the smell of her hair. When he peeked through a crack in the door to watch her walk along the hall, the rusty hinges almost gave him away, and for a moment Charlotte turned and he was sure he was caught. Thankfully, he had been able to close the door before she could notice where the sound had been. Then she was gone, and he'd retreated to his bedchamber.

James remained in his room, remembering all the things that were no longer his. Could never be his. It tore at his very soul. He turned his back on the window and marched from the room to his stepmother's chamber to check on her.

"How are you, mother?" he asked as he moved to sit at her bedside.

Her eyes fluttered open slightly and she smiled.

"Did you see her?"

James became still.

"I did."

"And?"

"And what, Stepmother?" James asked, pretending he did not understand.

She looked at him, reached her hand to touch his, and frowned.

"Do not be coy," she said. "You understand my meaning very well, I think."

"Do you mean to ask what I thought of her?" James continued, still pretending to be oblivious. "I thought she looked jolly well."

"Well?" Beatrice laughed lightly. "She looked much better than well."

James took a deep breath.

"Yes," he agreed. "She looked better than well. She looked very well indeed."

"She looked beautiful," Beatrice interjected.

James smiled lightly.

"Yes, mother. She looked beautiful. Even more so than when we knew one another as children."

She squeezed his hand. Her touch was so light it was like a feather brushing his skin.

"You can know each other again," she whispered.

"You know that cannot be," he protested. "And the reasons for it."

"James, dear..."

"She had a happy life, Stepmother. You heard her. She had what I could not give," James said. "Let it be left at that."

"You never gave her a chance," Beatrice replied. "You hid all these years, never allowing her to know the truth. Do you think she would have made the same choices if she knew you were alive?"

"You cannot know that."

"You do not know anything to the contrary," his stepmother insisted.

James was silent. It was true that he did not know. He

simply believed it, and it was that belief which he held on to. He could not give Charlotte what she deserved, not as he was now. Before, when he was his former self – whole – he would have given her the world. Now, he had to hide from it.

"James, you know Lady Charlotte. She is not like others," his stepmother persisted. "Why do you not give it a chance? Tell her the truth?"

He squeezed her hand gently and smiled.

"I would do anything for you, and you know that," he answered. "However, there are some things that are simply impossible. This is one of them."

"It seems impossible because you will not entertain the possibility," she countered. "You cannot tell me that part of you does not wish it."

He did not need to search his heart for the answer. It stood before him every day when he awoke. There was not a day since he had made his decision to let Charlotte go, that he had not doubted the rightness of it. He had regrets. He simply did not share them with anyone.

Charlotte was the love of his life. She was the only woman who had ever moved him, and he'd given her up to another. He was glad that her life was a happy one, and that she had a child she loved. He wanted nothing less for her.

It touched him to know that she still cared for him and kept him in her memory, but it also filled him with the pain of knowing that it could never be more than that.

"I have made my choice. She has her own life to lead now," he said solemnly.

"She is alone, James," Beatrice replied. "She needs someone to love her. And her child."

"She has her father and brother," he countered.

"You know that is not the same as a husband and father," she replied.

"And I, I'm afraid, am neither," James answered. "Have you forgotten the look on her father's face when he saw me again? I shall never forget it. He looked as if he'd seen a monster before him, and that is what I am to him. Nothing short of a creature from a nightmare."

Beatrice raised a hand to his face and James shied away from it.

"Your face does not make you a monster," she said weakly and placed her hand over his heart. "What is in here does."

"If only others could see what's inside and not my face, then all would be well. Life is not so simple or idyllic." He smiled lightly. "We must live in reality."

His stepmother saw little of the zigzag of scars that marred his face on every side, like the shell of a cracked egg, the result of a French bayonet's failed attempts to take his life. It might as well have done so, for all the life he'd had since.

"I will let you rest," he said, no longer able to bear the conversation about Charlotte and their lost love. He kissed his stepmother's forehead. "Sleep well. I will be here to have breakfast with you in the morning."

Beatrice smiled and nodded.

"Goodnight, son of my heart. Do consider my words. There is still love there," she stated. "In both of your hearts. Of that, I am quite certain."

James smiled a crooked smile and walked quietly from the room. He turned at the door and found his stepmother's eyes already closed in sleep. Her illness had taken so much out of her, every day, and he feared it worsening. His father had already lost one wife, and James did not think that he could bear the loss of another.

"Understand, Stepmother," he whispered. "I would have Charlotte live a life where all is beautiful – and that does not include a monster like me."

He closed the door behind him.

His father had paid handsomely for the household staff to remain silent about his presence. James did his part to avoid them at all costs. Their frightened looks and disturbed expressions were not ones he wished to experience in his daily life. It was bad enough that he had to look at himself. This was the only reminder he needed.

James found his meal in his bed chambers, as usual. He did not dine below. It was easier for everyone that way. Instead, he ate in his room once the main meal was over, and enjoyed his solitude.

He did not lack for entertainment, as one might think. He had his books and the newspapers, as well as Beatrice and his father for company. In addition, there were occasional visits from his old friend, William. The young man's continued friendship was the dearest relationship of his life, outside of Charlotte. He was glad he had not lost it when he had lost so much.

He ate his meal in silence, the taste of the food barely registering on his senses. He left the tray outside the door when he was finished, and collected his favorite book from his desk. He would read for a few hours and hope that sleep would then come quickly and peacefully for a change.

Since the war, James had suffered terrible nightmares, reliving the things he'd seen and endured. Some nights he didn't dare to close his eyes. But he fervently wished that tonight might be different, with the memory of the sight of Charlotte so close. Far better to dream of the woman he loved and could not have, than of the horrors of war.

He sat in his armchair by the window, with the lamp set on the ledge as he read. James had no trouble re-reading a good story and there were several that always entertained him. His books were his primary comfort late at night.

Sometime later, his father's voice called from the other side of the door.

"May I come in?"

James set the book aside. "Come in, Father."

John Watts walked into the room with a smile on his face. "And how are you this evening?"

"I am as well as can be expected under the circumstances, Father. Yourself?"

"I am more than well," he replied. "I have had a most delightful dinner." He looked at James. "Did you see Lady Charlotte?"

James should have known it was Charlotte, and not his well-being, that brought his father to visit him that night. His father was a thoughtful man, but on that night, the likelihood of that thoughtfulness outweighing his curiosity was slim.

"Indeed I did."

His father took a seat in the chair near him. "May I?"

James nodded.

"Did she not look lovely?"

James smiled slightly. He nodded. "Yes, Father. She did."

"She told me of her life," his father continued. "It was good for her at Bentonmere Park, but I am happy to have her back in this part of the country. I think it best, given her loss and the needs of her son. The boy will be a Marquess one day, you know, and he is already an Earl, although Lady Charlotte, as his guardian, deals with his affairs for now. It takes much effort to equip a young man for such responsibility."

James nodded. "That is right. Her husband was an Earl, and his father is a Marquess. I had almost forgotten."

He'd thought little of Charlotte's situation over the passing years, for only the woman herself interested him, and thinking of her with another man had been a torture he had chosen not to inflict upon himself.

"She could use the help," his father stated. He raised his eyebrows. James caught the look in his eyes.

"You believe I should be the one to give it?"

His father's smile broadened. "I believe it is time that you revealed yourself to her," he said solemnly. His father sat forward. "My boy, Lady Charlotte has returned to this county and back into our lives. What are the chances that this could happen? Does it not make you think that perhaps fate has engineered your reunion? That this may be an opportunity to reunite and find happiness together as you always wished?"

"Father, you and my dear stepmother are too alike," James replied, with a sad chuckle. "The answer I have for you is the same as the one I gave her. I will not change my mind. Charlotte's return has nothing to do with me. She is here for her son and family. She has no idea that I am here, nor should she ever have. Her life is better as it is – without me."

"Son..."

"She would only be sickened by me, and her boy frightened to look at me," James said, as the image of Charlotte's stunning features, twisted in disgust, flashed across his mind. "The boy would only run and hide from me. How could she stand to be in my presence?" He looked at his father's expression. He could see the empathy in his eyes. His father wanted his happiness, he knew that, but what he believed would make him so was not to be. He and Beatrice had to accept it. James had. "Father, I could not bear to see the expression of disgust on her face. That is something I could not live with."

His father reached out and touched his knee. "Can you live with her so close, and not being able to be together? It might not be what you think."

"It would be worse," James replied. "I could take that look from anyone but Charlotte. To see the derision and disgust in her eyes would be more than my life is worth. I would rather spare myself the torment and her the horror."

"James, you know that, more than anything, I was glad to have you back and alive. After believing you were dead for so long, your return was more than my heart could hope for at this stage of my life. Yet, there you were, scarred and tormented, but alive. And that, my boy, was all I could think of." His father smiled at him gently, but James could not bring himself to reciprocate. "I am sure that Lady Charlotte would feel the same," his father continued.

"I know that you mean well, Father, and that your words are meant to help me see the light, but you are wasting your time. Experience has taught me not to hope for anything. I wished to come home to a happy place, one of acceptance, where I could resume my life but it was not to be. I was forced, very quickly, to face the reality that people who look like me are not accepted in polite society."

"That girl was just young," his father protested. "Her reaction was... unfortunate."

"It was what I should have expected, father. She was not the first. I encountered the same response from others on my journey home. She was just the confirmation that my beliefs were true - England was no different, and I could not come home and live as I had before. My decision to remain in the shadows was for the best."

"Not in my mind," his father replied. "I miss having my son by my side. I miss being able to walk the square and talk with you, or visit our favorite establishments and see our old friends."

"They would not want me," James protested. "I am no longer what polite society wants. What they would want."

"You are what those who love you want, and from what Beatrice has told me, that love is not only held by her and myself, but by Lady Charlotte as well."

"Father, please," James said as he rushed to his feet. He turned from his father, torn by his words. "Why do you insist on this? Do you not understand how much it hurts to see her? How much I wish I did not look this way so that we could be together? But I do. This is who I am now. I cannot change."

"You cannot change your face, but you can change your future. It does not have to be alone. I want you to have what I had, the pleasure of raising a child of your own and having a wife at your side. Someone to love you in your old age."

"You must accept that it is not in my future. The Watts line will end with me," James said despondently. "I am sorry, Father. I wish it were not the case. I wish things were different, that I had never gone to that damnable war, but I did."

He heard his father take a long breath behind him.

"If that is what you believe," he said. "I will leave you now. Rest, my son. Perhaps the morning will bring with it new light to your life and your prospects."

James turned at his father's words.

"Goodnight, Father. Thank you. I know you mean well, and I am sorry that I cannot be as you want."

"All I want is for you to be happy again."

His father left the room and James with his thoughts. *If only life were so simple, and having Charlotte in his life again could be that easy*, he thought.

Then he shook his head. "Do not think it," he cautioned himself. "You will regret it later."

James reached into his pocket and retrieved the small locket hidden there. He opened the gold clasp and looked down at the small portrait that looked back at him. It was Charlotte, as she had been before the war. It was the last gift she'd given him. A keepsake to remember her.

"I will never tie you to one such as me," he said to the beautiful face in the locket. "You will not suffer torment as I do. You shall be happy, Charlotte. I will deny myself everything to see to it."

CHAPTER FOUR

Charlotte was pleased with herself, but she was even more pleased for Mrs. Watts, whose change in spirits had improved her physical health to the point that she could now be allowed outdoors.

"I have brought someone to meet you," she said, as she strolled towards Mrs. Watts, who was reclining on a chaise.

"A visitor?" Mrs. Watts questioned. Her face lit up immediately, as her eyes fell upon Charlotte's son. "Oh my! Is this George?"

"Yes, it is," Charlotte said, beaming proudly.

She took the stuffed bear from her son's grasp. It was his favorite toy and the one without which George could not sleep.

"Georgie, please greet Mrs. Watts."

Her son walked toward the older woman and bowed his head solemnly. "Good day, Mrs. Watts," he said with a strangely adult manner.

"He is darling," Mrs. Watts sang. "Now, George," she

said, turning to George, who was smiling at her happiness. "You will be quite the imposing Marquess someday."

"Yes ma'am, I shall do my utmost," he said, still solemn.

"It is my dearest wish that it be so," Charlotte replied. "His father would expect it."

She took her son by the hand and led him to the blanket that was spread over the grass.

Mrs. Watts smiled at the pair.

"I am so very pleased to see you here. I was hoping you would visit. I had this picnic prepared in hopes of it."

"You planned for us?" Charlotte chuckled. A broad smile lingered on her face. "And here I was thinking I would surprise you. But no matter. I am glad you did."

"And I am glad you came," Mrs. Watts replied. "I wanted for company."

"Then all the better, my dear Mrs. Watts!" said Charlotte. "George and I shall be all the company you need until Mr. Watts returns."

Charlotte pulled her son onto her lap and popped a kiss on his chubby cheek. The child giggled and squirmed in place. Mrs. Watts sat up on the chaise longue, her eyes fixed happily on them.

"How have you adjusted to being home again?"

Charlotte took a deep breath before she answered. "As well as could be expected, I suppose," she admitted. "Father makes it difficult to live one's life."

Her former governess nodded. "I expected it would be so. He has always had a plan for everyone under his roof. He had his plans for me, but I defied them." She giggled.

Charlotte looked at Mrs. Watts, perplexed. "A plan for you?"

The older woman laughed. "Why yes. Did he never tell you? There was a gentleman of his acquaintance who was in need of a wife, and whose interests aligned with his. He hoped he could force the two of us together to seal the deal."

"Whatever happened?" Charlotte asked, incredulous. She'd had no idea that her father had attempted such a plan, and Mrs. Watts had never mentioned it before then. And she was somewhat horrified at the machinations of her father, for whom she had the greatest respect, but the greatest fear that something similar should happen to her.

"Oh, my dear," laughed Mrs. Watts merrily. "I was in love. Dear Mr. Watts and I were already acquainted through his work with your father, and he began courting me in secret. Neither of us wanted our private understanding made known until we were certain of what might come of it. The moment we were sure that marriage was a certainty in our future, we made the announcement to your father."

Charlotte looked at her keenly. "And how did Father take it?"

The question elicited a deep chuckle from the woman before her. It made Charlotte smile to hear the sweet timbre return to her former governess's voice. She hardly seemed ill at all, except for an occasional errant cough.

"He did his best to hide his displeasure, of course, being the gentleman he is. He had great respect for me and Mr. Watts, and although we caused a problem in his plans, he would not deny that our union was a great benefit to us both." She nodded lightly. "I believe he was happy for us in the end, though he did not relish the loss of my services to you and William."

"It was no trouble to us," Charlotte interjected. "We were glad that you had found happiness with Mr. Watts. It is true we missed you terribly, but I was hardly a child and William even less so. Besides, it allowed us to become better acquainted with James. If you had not married Mr. Watts, I wonder if we should ever have become friends. Father had never allowed us to come to Watton Hall before that, and Mr. Watts never brought James to Caldor."

Mrs. Watts smiled broadly. "Then I believe that my marriage benefitted all of us more than I originally thought."

"Quite," Charlotte agreed. She patted her lap, arranging her skirts just as George began to fidget, trying to extricate himself from her grasp. He was not a child who kept still for long at a time, and Charlotte was used to his activeness. Still, she tried to keep him as calm as possible, given Mrs. Watts' condition.

"He is certainly an active boy," Mrs. Watts commented.

"Very," Charlotte confirmed as she released George.

"I am, ma'am, that's for certain," he said to Mrs. Watts. He immediately ran for the nearest bush and

Charlotte scrambled to her feet after him, trying to catch him on the other side of the bush.

Her actions were taken as the instigation of a game by her son, who ran even faster to keep from her grasp. He laughed harder, a small squeal of delight leaping from his lips as he tried to keep ahead of her. Charlotte laughed with him.

Laughter became the song of the party as Mrs. Watts amused herself with their playful display.

"Run, Georgie!" she encouraged him. "Keep running!"

"You'll never catch me, Mama," he squealed merrily, as he ran as fast as his little legs would carry him.

Charlotte eventually caught up to her son, plucked the boy from his feet, and spun him in the air as his delighted laughter rose to a crescendo. She hugged him close as her laughter subsided. Turning back towards the blanket, her eyes scanned across the façade of the house, and suddenly her laughter stopped.

It was only a moment, a glimpse in an upper window, but Charlotte was sure that she had not imagined it. There had been a man standing, looking through the glass. She was sure of it, but then he was gone. It was James' old bedroom window, she was sure of that too. She stared up at the window for several moments, hoping that the individual would present himself again. He did not.

"Charlotte, is everything alright? You look as if you have seen a ghost!" cried Mrs. Watts in alarm, her brow furrowed slightly.

Charlotte turned her attention to the older woman. "I think I may have, I warrant."

Mrs. Watts looked at her quizzically. "A ghost? At Watton Hall?"

"I thought... that is... I am sure I saw someone looking down from the upstairs window. James' bedroom window, to be specific," Charlotte declared.

Mrs. Watts' eyes grew large. "Did you? How strange? There is no one up there."

The denial was clear, but there was something in Mrs. Watts' tone which made Charlotte wonder if her response was genuine. Could it be that she did have a guest, someone she did not wish Charlotte to know about? She decided to press the matter. Mrs. Watts had never kept secrets from her before, and she doubted she would now.

"Are you sure? I know that I saw someone. I'm certain of it. A man."

"Dear dear, no. There is no one," Mrs. Watts quickly assured her. "The only man who works in the house is the footman, and he has no reason to be upstairs. You must have been seeing things."

Charlotte frowned. "It is not just that," she admitted. Until then she'd refrained from speaking to Mrs. Watts of her experiences, but now she felt the time was at hand.

"Is there something you have not told me?" asked Mrs. Watts, uneasily.

"In fact, there is," Charlotte answered. She lowered herself onto the blanket once more and reached for a biscuit to settle George, who had become restless no doubt sensing his mother's discomfort.

"What is it?" said Mrs. Watts, with concern, leaning forward.

Charlotte felt slightly silly mentioning it. Mrs. Watts would likely only think it was her imagination, but she was sure there was someone in the house – someone who was watching her.

"I've had several strange experiences since my first visit," she said slowly. "When I am in the house I feel as though someone is watching me. Sometimes I think I hear a door open or close behind me, but when I look or call, there is no one there. Now, today, the figure in the window. It was watching me. I am quite sure of it."

Mrs. Watts' gaze left her face and diverted to the shrubbery as she once again denied there being anyone. Charlotte sat stunned. Mrs. Watts was hiding something from her. *But why?*

Charlotte began to wonder. These strange experiences. Mrs. Watts' denials. Her father's insistence that she not visit, and William's agreement. Were they all hiding something from her?

The three of them continued to spend time in the garden until the sun began to wane. Charlotte was kind to Mrs. Watts, and Mrs. Watts was evasive.

"Look at the time. I really must go," Charlotte said. "George must have his dinner and get to bed."

Mrs. Watts rose slowly from the chaise. "I shall have your carriage brought around, but you must promise to come again soon," she said and stepped forward to embrace her. "And you must bring that delightful boy with you. He is such a joy."

"I will do so," Charlotte promised with a smile. She held tightly onto George's hand.

Mrs. Watts beckoned to the maid who stood nearby

and sent her with the message for the coachman before the trio proceeded slowly inside. Her nurse came to give aid, as she was still very weak and could not walk on her own for any great distance.

They walked to the entry hall, where Mrs. Watts bid them farewell and waited with them until their carriage appeared. Her nurse brought a chair for her to sit on as they waited. She remained at the door until they were tucked safely inside the carriage, and then the door closed behind her.

"Drive on," Charlotte instructed. She nestled George into her side. The lively boy was fatigued from all of that running about and was now listless as sleep began to overwhelm him. There was nothing like running to weary a child, and George had run more than his share that day.

"Bear," George said irritably. "Bear!"

They'd forgotten it. They were only a mile or so from the house. It was no trouble to return and retrieve the toy.

"Coachman, turn around, please. I have forgotten something."

"Yes, my Lady," said the coachman.

They drove back to Watton Hall, George becoming more irritable by the moment as sleepiness made him miserable.

"All right, George. Settle yourself. You will have your bear shortly," she soothed as she gently patted his head. "Hush."

The carriage stopped outside Watton Hall and Charlotte stepped down quickly, opening the door herself and eschewing the steps. She did not wait for the coachman or footman to let them down for her. It would only take a moment.

"Wait here," she instructed the footman. "Watch over my son."

The footman nodded and stood by the closed carriage door as she rushed up the stairs to the house. She could hear George whimpering behind her as she knocked. The housekeeper answered.

"I have returned, Mrs. Boyle," she said with a smile. "I have forgotten my son's toy. Do you know where it might be?"

"Yes, Lady Charlotte. I put the toy in the parlor for safekeeping, until your next visit. But of course, I can get it for you."

"There is no need for you to bother yourself," Charlotte replied cheerfully. "You have your responsibilities. I can find it myself." She chuckled. "I do remember the way. It has not been so terribly long."

Mrs. Boyle smiled. She had served the Watts family for as long as Charlotte had known Mr. Watts. She had been there to witness her childhood, and now she had no opposition to Charlotte wandering the house on her own. She had done so many times in the past. "Very well. Should I tell the Mistress that you are here?"

"No," Charlotte said quickly. "There's no need to trouble her. I am leaving again presently."

"Will you let yourself out?"

"Yes, of course. You need not trouble yourself over me. It can be as old times," she mused.

"Ay, and they were very good times, and all," said Mrs. Boyle. "If this is what you wish, my Lady, I shall carry on." Mrs. Boyle curtsied and tottered away to complete her chores.

Charlotte walked toward the parlor. Her steps were brisk, for she knew that George must be making a frightful fuss with her away from him. She did not want to leave the poor footman with such a burden for long. George was her responsibility.

She rushed into the room and found the bear nestled amongst the cushions on the couch. She grabbed it quickly and hurried back. She was halfway to the entry when the sound of music caught her attention. Her steps stopped immediately.

The tune was undeniable. Charlotte would recognize it anywhere. It was a piece she had heard thousands of times over the years. It was James' favorite song, "Sweet is the Vale" by Georgiana Cavendish, the Duchess of Devonshire, and he would have her play it for him every time she visited the house. On rare occasions, he would play it for her, but he always preferred her playing. She could feel the music come out of her as she heard the pianoforte elicit the melody.

Memories filled her mind, and Charlotte found that she could not move from where she stood. "Sweet is the vale where innocence resides," she murmured, remembering the beautiful melody she used to sing to James. She lingered, immobile for several long seconds before her feet drew her toward the music and away from the front door.

It was a siren's song and she a hapless sailor. She wandered the halls to the music room, where the pianoforte was kept. She stood outside the door, the melodious tune wafting from the other side. She hesitated. Should she go in, or stay and listen longer?

She continued singing softly to the distant piano music. "Blessed is the cot where virtue dwells," she sang. And almost without her will, her feet moved of their own accord and soon her hands reached for the handle of the door. She opened it quietly, not wanting to disturb whoever was playing. She did not want to break the spell of the music, and the sweet memories it elicited.

Charlotte stood in wonder and watched the man who sat at the instrument. The way he was seated. The song he was playing. She continued singing, slightly louder this time, mesmerized by the beauty of the song and the memories.

"Where harmless love untaught presides," she sang. But she was torn, because the way his hands moved over the keys, with such confidence and grace, it was uncannily like James. Charlotte's eyes filled with tears. Her voice caught, and she ceased her singing.

It was a colossal and terrible joke. It had to be. Whoever this man was, either he had no idea what the song meant to her, or he was doing this deliberately to bait her. Charlotte did not know which was worse. She wanted to say something but her tongue betrayed her.

She lingered at the back of the room, listening to the rumbles of the man as he sang the words and played on the pianoforte. "Secure from flatteries' baneful spells," he sang. Charlotte shook her head; it was as though this unknown man had taken her heart, turned it to music, and had begun relishing her happy memories. "This is the spot, and here I wish to live," sang the voice, so similar in timbre to James, but somehow broken. "Despising all that wealth and pow'r can give," he continued in the broken beauty. This was a duet and she still knew every word and every note of it. But the horror of this macabre memory torn from her past before her lover had died was too much for her. She was frozen to the spot as he finished singing and played the ending of the song.

She had not intended to stay until the end, but she did, and soon found herself faced with making her intrusion known. She could not do that, her son was waiting. She turned to leave, but the pianist moved faster. He ended the song with an angry slam of his fists against the keys, and then abruptly stood and turned, coming face-to-face with her.

The toy fell from her hand as Charlotte stood transfixed. Her eyes grew large. Her heart quickened, and her mind fogged in disbelief. It could not be. Her eyes were deceiving her. It was the magic of the music. She was seeing things.

Charlotte stepped forward. The man stepped back, knocking into the bench behind him. Charlotte began to tremble.

"It cannot be," she whispered. "James?"

The look in his eyes was answer enough. The shock and recognition of his name. It was not her imagination. It was him.

The tears spilled uncontrollably from her eyes as Charlotte ran toward James. She wrapped her arms tightly around his neck, calling his name repeatedly as if the act would solidify the truth and assure her that she was not about to wake from a dream.

"James, how is this possible? How are you here?" She pulled back to look at him. "Where have you been? Why did you not contact me? I do not understand. How are you alive?"

The tears continued to flow as Charlotte buried her face in James' breast. She held his lapels as if they anchored her to the earth. Her legs felt weak and she was sure her knees would give out if she did not have his clothing to hold onto.

She wanted him to hold her. She expected it, but he did not.

James did not answer. His hands remained fixed at his sides as he remained silent. Charlotte continued her questioning, unable to stop herself.

She wanted to know how it was possible. She needed to know everything.

Her James was alive. How many knew? Why was it a secret?

"I have missed you," she whispered. "So very much."

CHAPTER FIVE

Why was she there? She was supposed to be gone. James had waited until the carriage was out of sight before he left the confines of his room, to ensure that he would avoid Charlotte, and yet here she was.

Everything within told him to run away, but his heart held him fast. He was sure she would run at the sight of him, but again he was mistaken. Instead, she stood so still, and when she said his name it felt as if everything in the world stopped at the sound.

Something inside of him stilled completely. For so long, he had only heard his name on her lips in dreams, but to hear it in person was more wonderful. It captured him, locked him in place, and arrested his good sense. The sense which would have told him to escape before another word was spoken.

He was still transfixed when she ran to him, throwing her arms around his neck and holding him tightly. His hands couldn't move to hold her, though they desperately wanted to. He was too stunned to react, mortified. She was there, within grasp, looking at him without fear or disgust. How could this be?

She would run, isn't that what you believed? She would run away at the sight of you? So why does she hold you now? Why does she cry and call your name?

His mind was conflicted.

James had believed for so long that what he thought was true, and that Charlotte would reject him as others had before. Now, he was left in bewilderment, torn between misconception and reality.

Charlotte launched a thousand questions at him, but James had no words to answer her. His mind was blank. He gasped like a fish out of water. Never, in his wildest dreams had he ever imagined that Charlotte could react in such a way, or that he would be faced with such an implausible meeting. He'd done everything he could to prevent this, everything he'd imagined would work to prevent them from ever seeing each other again. But it seemed his best-laid plans were for nothing, and in the end, they were together once more.

The longer she held him, the more he lost himself in her embrace. The scent of her hair wafted up to his nostrils and filled his senses with delightful memories. Precious memories. His hands rose involuntarily to hold her but his fingers curled into fists with the effort of preventing the action. He could not hold her. She was not his. She never would be. Still, he allowed himself to be seduced by the moment, by her lingering embrace, her sweet scent, and the gentle timbre of her tears.

For only a moment; he would allow himself only a

moment. A moment to linger in the joy of the sensations he was feeling before they would be gone forever.

James, you will not last if you continue in this. You must extricate yourself from her. Do it now!

Immediately his hands shot up and took hold of Charlotte's arms, forcing her away from him, and putting her at arm's length. He allowed himself one last look before he attempted to make his escape, only to find his plan foiled by Charlotte's quick thinking. She stepped into his path and blocked his way.

"James, where you going? Why won't you answer me?" Charlotte tearfully insisted.

He tried to avoid her eyes. All hope was lost if he dared meet those eyes. Once again, he attempted to escape and was foiled a second time. He raised his voice.

"Let me be."

Deep lines wrinkled Charlotte's forehead as she looked at him in absolute astonishment.

"No!" she insisted. "You must tell me how this can be? What happened to you? All these years I thought you were dead and yet here you are. Why did you never come to me? Why did you never contact me? Why did I never know?"

The more she spoke the more her words sounded like pleas.

Pleas that tore at his heart and pulled every string. She attempted to touch him, but James could ill afford such an interaction. The light was dim, he told himself. The low candlelight was masking his scars, his horror. And he could not let her see his misshapen face. He deflected her and stepped away to ensure that distance remained between them.

It has to be this way. "I have no explanation to give," he replied coldly. He still avoided her eyes and folded his arms behind his back.

"No explanation?" Charlotte shook her head in bewilderment. "How can you say that?"

"I am sorry, Lady Benton, but I have no answers for you. What I would say would only cause you hurt. It would be best for you if you left this house now, and did not return to it." His voice was cracked and broken, but unmistakably James.

He wanted to run, to run away from the words he had to utter. The feelings that threatened his resolve and the urge to look at her beautiful face at every moment. But there was no escape. Charlotte would never be satisfied to simply be dismissed. She was persistent. She would not leave without answers. Only the cruelest of measures would make her go. Measures he was willing to take.

She had a right to her questions, there was no doubting it, but James could not give her what she yearned for. He could not give her what she needed. How could he admit the lies he'd told, and forced others to tell? How could he admit to her that for all of these years he'd been alive and well, and had allowed her to live her own life without him? She would never understand.

She did not bear his scars or his memories. She had not worn the pain of the past few years as he had. His actions had allowed her to live a happy life with her husband and child. It was the life that James would have had with her, the life he gave away to another. He did not regret that. He would not. Therefore, he could not answer her.

He tried to rush past her, but she grabbed the hem of his waistcoat and called out his name in such a pitiful cry that he found his muscles seized. He closed his eyes against the sound as it pierced through him.

"James!"

He should have pulled away, but he did not. An aching hunger for what he'd lost caused him to slowly turn to face her. The sight that met him shattered him, as he met her gaze and the tortured look on her face.

Tears dampened her red cheeks as more inundated her eyes. Her lips quivered and she looked at him with such pain in her gaze that it closed his throat, preventing him from speaking. Her hand lingered on his clothing.

Everything in him wanted to hold her and give her comfort, to make better the wrong he had done her, and all of the years before it, but he could not allow himself to.

The sound of rushing footsteps and the sudden opening of the door behind him broke his torment. His father burst into the room, the declaration of Charlotte's return on his lips. It had come too late.

"I am afraid you are too late with your news, Father," James replied acidly, as he turned to him. "Lady Benton is here."

Charlotte's hand fell away from his clothing at the impersonal address. She turned with disbelieving eyes to his father.

"Why did you not tell me? Did Mrs. Watts know as well?" she accused.

His father looked to him for help, but what help could he give? He could not tell her the truth, not after so long. It was best for things to stay as they were. His father must have recognized that James would not help him, and chose to address Charlotte himself.

"My dear, please try to understand..."

His father began to speak, but James could not let him. He could not allow Charlotte to hold any animosity toward his father or stepmother because of him. He would shoulder the complete blame himself. After all, it was his choices that were the cause of everything.

"I asked him to withhold this news from you," James stated bluntly. He steeled himself and met Charlotte's eyes. "I did not wish him to make you aware of my presence."

"But why?" she asked pitifully.

His father stepped toward Charlotte with a proffered handkerchief, which she took, and promptly dabbed her eyes and wiped her nose. His father's gaze met his, and he knew, for a certainty, what he was thinking, but James would not do as he wished.

"I never wanted you to know I was still alive. I wanted you to believe I was dead and to move on with your life. I needed to escape you, Lady Benton," he began his lie, and casually strolled around her.

"While I was away, I realized that the life we wanted together could never be. We could never be happy, and therefore it was a useless endeavor to even pursue it. I took the opportunity to extricate myself from your life and had no intention of ever reuniting with you. It was my greatest pleasure when you left this county and allowed me more room and freedom to live my life here. In secret, yes, but still the life I chose."

Charlotte looked as if he had stabbed her.

"Do you mean to say you pretended to be dead to escape me?"

The lie was bitter on his lips as he uttered it. He turned the knife.

"Yes."

His father looked at him but James shook his head lightly to keep him silent. He had made his choice, and this was his decision. He had to make Charlotte leave and never want to return. The only way was to hurt her to save her, to save her from herself and the life that she would live being in his company once again. It was a hard life for him, now that he was so scarred, and he would not allow her to endure such hardship, even if it was only to be his friend.

"You went to such lengths to be rid of me? Years of lies and deceit just to say you did not want me anymore?" Her nose flared and she looked at him squarely. "I do not believe it! I will not believe it! I cannot believe it!"

"You must believe it," James answered solemnly, his face still turned from her. He lifted his chin and looked upon her coldly. "I realized while I was there, that I had never loved you, Charlotte. These injuries I suffered only helped me to see things more clearly," he said, turning to her, and expecting her to recoil in horror. "I looked at the prospects for my future, and I realized that there was no room for you in it. The woman I needed was a much different woman, and you simply would not suffice. I was all the happier when you finally married Malcolm Tate." He made his voice colder. His words meant to injure. "I was happy to see how quickly you forgot me."

"I never forgot..."

"I do not want to hear it," James interrupted sharply, then softened it to an indifferent tone. He had not noticed the look of love on her face. "My only wish now, Lady Benton, is for you to leave this house and never come back. I know that you and my stepmother share a fondness for one another and that such fondness might encourage you to return to this house on more frequent occasions. I will caution you against it. Though her health has improved with your visits, I believe the conflict between us would only retard her progress. Therefore, it would be best that you did not return. I am sure she will find her way to meet you when she is well enough. Now please, would you please leave?"

James bowed his head curtly, turned on his heel, and rushed out of the room. He could hear Charlotte trying to come after him and his father's attempts to prevent her. He did not turn around. He marched to his room and shut the door, locking it behind him immediately. Then, as if every ounce of his energy had been expended on delivering those lies, his legs gave way and he found himself seated upon the floor.

What a pitiful thing it was for them to meet again under such circumstances. What a cruel game fate had played against him. His hands balled into fists at his sides, and he slammed them against the floor as tears stung his eyes.

"Music," he said with hatred in his voice. "Of course, this sentimental song would be my undoing!" Tears, which he refused to shed, gathered in his voice. He had never lied directly to her before, yet today, he had done nothing but lie.

His heart ached and his head felt as if it would split in two under the pressure and strain of what he had done. The grief he felt in his heart was no less than what she felt now, he was sure. To hurt Charlotte was to hurt himself and he had done it for her benefit, although he knew she would never understand, and might never believe it.

"Why did she have to come back? Why did I have to be in that damnable room as I was playing that song?"

James did not doubt it was the music he'd played that had lured her in and caused her to find him. It was his favorite song, "Sweet is the Vale" and one he had always played for her, or with her, or had her play, whenever they were together. He'd allowed his melancholy memories to take him to a place he should never have gone, and because of it, he had drawn into the room the one person he'd hoped would never see him again.

He stayed slumped on the floor for what seemed like an eternity. The sun dipped lower on the horizon and the room slowly darkened. It was almost black by the time his father's knock intruded on his misery.

"James, I wish to speak to you."

He'd expected as much. James stood, unlocked the door, and turned away before his father could enter. He walked to the lamp by his bed and lit it, and then to the one on his writing desk. Then, he turned to face his father.

"Yes?"

John Watts shook his head in disappointment and disbelief. "What have you done?"

"What I had to," James replied heavily. "I had to make her leave. It was the only way."

Pain was in his father's eyes as he looked at him.

"I do not think such cruelty was necessary."

James shook his head. "You do not know Charlotte as I do. She would have stayed and pressed me for answers until she got them." He met his father's eyes with a weary gaze. "I would not have been able to endure it."

"Then why not explain to her? Tell her the truth?" his father protested.

"Father, you do not understand," James said more emphatically. "The truth would not help. She would keep coming back. She would keep pressing me. She would want to work her way back into my life, and I cannot have that. I will not have that. I will not have her see the wretched creature I have become."

His father stepped toward him and laid a gentle hand on his shoulder. "Son, did she even mention your scars? Or is it you who call yourself a monster?"

James looked at his father in silence for several long seconds.

"She did not even seem to notice," said James bitterly. "And I do not know if it was better or worse that she did not."

"What do you mean?"

"I expected her to," James explained. "I was prepared

for it and when it did not come, I was completely undone. It made no sense to me. She made no sense to me. How can she ignore the first and most obvious thing about me? My face, my disfigured visage." He was utterly bewildered by it still. "How could she not mention my face? It is all I ever see. All anyone ever sees."

His father smiled at him with great sympathy. "No, James, it is what you see, but it is not necessarily what everyone else sees. When you first came home, your scars mattered little compared to the fact that you were alive, and they mean even less to me now. I tried to tell you that Lady Charlotte would feel the same way. Your stepmother tried to tell you so too, but you would not listen. You believed what you wanted to believe because it was easiest. It allowed you to hide, and never to face the fact that you no longer feel as if you are the man you were before the war. Lady Charlotte did not abandon you because of your face, James. It was you who abandoned her."

His father's words were like a bolt of lightning to his soul. The truth pierced him to the bone and left him utterly speechless. His father lingered with him for a moment longer before he turned and left the room. James remained with his thoughts.

He lowered himself onto the edge of his bed and looked at the flickering lamplight as he tried to understand how his life had come to such a point. Everything he'd thought he knew now seemed wrong. Had he miscalculated? Had he imposed his fear and rejection of himself upon Charlotte, believing that what he felt about himself was what she would too?

"What does it matter? What has been done is done, and there is no changing it."

Whatever the truth was, it mattered little now. He was sure his words had been successful in breaking Charlotte's heart, so she would not break his.

I have no heart left to break.

CHAPTER SIX

Charlotte tried to go after James but found herself held fast by his father's gentle but firm grip. She looked at Mr. Watts. Why was he stopping her? Did he not understand that she had to find James? She had to know why?

"It is no use," Mr. Watts told her. "Let him go."

Charlotte shook her head in disbelief. None of this made sense. James was alive and wanted nothing to do with her? It could not be true. She wanted answers. She needed answers. If James would not provide them, then his father would. He was the only person who could give her what she needed.

"Please, Mr. Watts, tell me everything."

The older man looked at her with pity as he answered.

"It is not my story to tell. I do wish that I could say more, but I cannot. If James will not utter it, then I cannot presume to say anything. It would be a betrayal."

"But surely you can tell me?" she insisted. "After all these years?"

He took her hand and patted her knuckles gently.

"You have had a shock. I think you'd better sit down."

Mr. Watts led her to a nearby chair and Charlotte lowered herself into it.

"I will ask a servant to bring you some water," he insisted.

"No, thank you," Charlotte replied. "I would much rather have answers than water, and if I cannot have those, I want the latter even less."

Mr. Watts nodded his head in understanding and sat nearby, simply giving her the space to think.

Charlotte's head was spinning and her heart was racing. How many years had she dreamt that James' death was a lie and that he would come back to her? How many nights had she dreamt of their joyous reunion, only to wake to the fact that it was just a fantasy? Now to see him, and to hear such terrible words from him, tore her apart. The belief she had lived with all these years, the certainty that she would have been happier with him, was all a lie. It was false. He did not want her.

It cannot be. James loved you. No matter what he says, you know that he loved you and you loved him.

Her eyes shot to his father's face.

"What happened to him?"

Again, Mr. Watts refused to answer. He shook his head and looked at her with gentle kindness.

"He came back from the war a different man. That is all I can tell you."

He lowered his head and shifted his gaze. Charlotte

leaned forward and took hold of Mr. Watts' hands. He lifted his eyes and met her gaze.

"But he came back," she said gently. She forced a small smile. "He is alive."

Mr. Watts nodded silently. However, his expression soon fell.

"My dear, I must ask you to forgive me and my family for what you have just suffered." Charlotte looked at him, confused. "My son spoke to you in the most abominable of ways, and I am deeply saddened and regretful of it. You, of all people, have been a cherished friend and acquaintance to our family, and for him to treat you in such a pitiless manner is most unsettling."

"You have done nothing that would require forgiveness," Charlotte answered. "It was not you but James who said these things."

She could not continue. It hurt too much.

"I know, but I feel it is my responsibility to apologize for his actions. After all, he is my son," Mr. Watts replied. He raised his eyes. "And I must ask you not to tell his stepmother of this incident. I fear that what he said is true, and being informed of what transpired this evening would only grieve Beatrice. I fear it would set back the improvement of her health."

Thoughts of her former governess and the progress she'd made over the weeks only made Charlotte's heart heavier. She could not bear to be the one responsible for any slowing in her improvement. However, it wasn't fair of James to ask her to stay away, given the fact that much of Beatrice's progress was due to Charlotte's presence.

"He is being terribly unfair," she protested. "To ask

me never to return here? Watton Hall has been a second home to me since I was a girl. You and Mrs. Watts are like family to me. It is unfair to ask me to stay away."

"I agree. It was an unfair request, and I hope that you will not abide by it," Mr. Watts said firmly. "James might be my son, but he is not lord and master of this house. I am. You, my dear, are always welcome here."

He smiled at her in a kindly way.

Mr. Watts' words were punctuated by the closing of his hand around hers and a gentle but firm squeeze around her fingers. Charlotte smiled sadly and nodded her understanding.

"Thank you, Mr. Watts."

"Dry your tears and calm yourself," he instructed. "Your son is waiting for you."

In the shock of it all Charlotte had almost forgotten poor George waiting for her in the carriage, and the helpless footman left with the task of watching over him.

"My goodness, you are right!" She quickly dried her face and returned the handkerchief to Mr. Watts. She leaped to her feet, retrieved her son's toy, and then looked over her shoulder at the older man who still watched her with concern. "Thank you for everything you've done and said. I shall be going now."

Mr. Watts tucked his handkerchief back into his top pocket and followed her from the room.

"It was nothing. Let me see you to the carriage."

They walked together out of the house and to the carriage, where her dear son was making the footman positively miserable if the expression on his face was any indication. She apologized for the delay as she stepped up into the carriage.

"'Twas nothing, Lady Benton," the coachman replied.

Charlotte was sure he was just being kind, but she was grateful for it. She pulled George onto her lap and cradled him against her chest.

"Hush George," she said soothingly as the carriage pulled away. "I am here and so is your bear."

"Oh, thank you, Mama," said George. The child took his toy and hugged it to him, his tired eyes closing almost immediately at the comfort he found in the small item. She watched him closely as he slowly fell asleep, and gently brushed the strands of hair from his forehead.

I once wondered what my child would look like if James had lived. Now, I look at you and wonder it again. You would like James. I believe that he would like you if only he would allow it.

She raised her eyes to look out of the window as tears began to sting them.

Why did he do this? It makes no sense. I cannot believe what he said. There must be more to this.

She closed her eyes until they reached Caldor House.

CHARLOTTE COULD HARDLY CONTAIN herself as the carriage stopped outside her home. She could only imagine what her brother and father would say when they found out the news that James was alive. They would no doubt be as shocked as she was.

Mrs. White was waiting on the step when they arrived. Charlotte suspected she had been watching from the window, waiting for her precious charge to return. Mrs. White loved George as if he were her own. She had watched over him since his birth, and, as she had no children of her own, Charlotte allowed her overprotectiveness.

"I was beginning to worry," the nurse said as she took George from her. She nestled the boy against her shoulder. He stirred but did not wake.

"We were delayed, but we are here now. Please see George to his bed. I must find my father and brother. If George wakes give him some warm milk, a light snack, and get him back to sleep, he's had a very energetic day."

"Yes, Lady Benton."

Charlotte ran up the front stairs before Mrs. White, and in the door moments later.

"Have you seen my father and brother?" she asked the housekeeper, who was passing through the entryway.

"They are here somewhere, perhaps in your father's study," Mrs. Boyle replied. "I will send a footman to discover their location for you."

"There is no need for that," Charlotte replied. She completely ignored the fact that George was sleeping and allowed her voice to be heard almost throughout the house, raising it in a most unladylike fashion. "Father! Brother!"

Again and again, she called until they answered.

Her father's disgruntled face appeared on the balcony above her. He looked down angrily.

"What is all this noise about? Charlotte, why are you behaving like a fishmonger's wife?"

She ignored him. Fishmonger's wife or not, what she had to say could not wait to be heard, and once she had told them, she was sure that they would forgive her impoliteness.

Her brother appeared in the corridor near her and rushed to her side, as her father continued to stare down at her disapprovingly.

"What is it, Charlotte? Has something happened?" Concern filled his voice.

She held onto her brother as intermingled dismay and happiness washed over her again.

"James Watts is alive!" Charlotte waited for their shocked expressions and words of disbelief at her declaration, but nothing came. Instead, they looked at one another silently, their expressions grave. It was then that the truth dawned on her. "You knew? Is that why you did not want me to go to Watton Hall? Is it?"

Her brother looked at her, and his jaw slackened as he tried to find the words to answer her. He need not have. His silence spoke volumes.

"Yes," her father admitted as he descended the stairs to meet them. "I see that, after all of this time, he has done a poor job of concealing himself."

His words were so dismissive that they left Charlotte dumbfounded.

"Father," William interjected.

"What?" he retorted. "Am I expected to feel some way about what I have said? He asked us to keep the truth secret, and yet he reveals himself the moment Charlotte returns. It was a waste of my time and energy if he was so easily swayed to go back on his word when staying hidden was by far the wisest choice he could have made."

Her father leveled a stern look at those of the household staff who had gathered at the sound of her calls. Immediately, they retreated to safety, none wanting to bear her father's ire.

"Now, if we could take this conversation into a more private area, I would be grateful."

Charlotte was still stunned as her father turned and walked toward his study. She looked at her brother for help.

"We'd better follow him," he instructed.

"But William..."

"Trust me, Charlotte, it is better to discuss this elsewhere," her brother insisted. Charlotte, after a moment's thought, agreed and walked with him, following their father.

Her father's words replayed in her head as she walked. He thought that what James had done was the best choice? How could he say such a thing?

"Father," she stated the moment the door of the study was closed behind them. "What did you mean just now? When you said you think James was right in his choice?"

Her father sat and clasped his hands on his desk as he stared at her. He looked as if he was ready for a business meeting, not to have a discussion with his children about something so momentous.

"Charlotte, do be seated," he instructed. "I can see that you have been unsettled by this revelation. You'd best sit before you fall."

William helped her to a seat and Charlotte reluctantly did as her father had requested.

"Please, Father," she said. "Explain," she demanded the moment she was seated.

"You are not blind, Charlotte. Surely you saw his face?"

Charlotte reflected on her meeting with James. She'd hardly noticed his face. The shock that James was alive had superseded any consideration of the state that he was in. She focused her mind on him and for the first time saw, in her memory of that moment, his marred features. *He looked so pitiful.*

"What of it?" she questioned.

"One who looks as he does is best out of the sight of society," her father answered bluntly. "I almost lost my composure when I first saw him. Thankfully, I have a strong constitution."

There was a note of pride in the statement.

"Father! James went to war. He was obviously wounded. How can you say that about him?" Charlotte protested.

Her father got to his feet and clasped the buttons on his coat. "Charlotte, be practical. A man who looks as James Watts does is not the kind that society accepts. Flawed as you may think it, unfair even, it is the way of things, and we are not here to change such things but to deal with reality. Captain James Watts is no longer a man who can easily be accepted in good company, war hero or not." He stepped out from behind his desk and stood before her. "You would likewise be unwelcome if you were to accompany him. Therefore, James' decision to keep himself apart from you was a wise one. One I agree with. I only wish he had kept his word. Now, if this matter is settled, I have to see to my new stallion. He was getting a new shoe and I must ensure that the work was properly done. He is worth far too much to risk him being lamed."

Charlotte could not believe her father's words. She was still unable to speak as she watched him leave the room, and William stood silently by. He stirred when her gaze fell on him.

"Do you share Father's feelings? Is that why you tried to keep me away?" she demanded.

"No, I do not," William answered quickly. "Never! James is my friend. He always has been. What I did was because..."

His words faltered.

"Because?"

"Because I saw what the war had done to him," William answered.

"But you told him I was coming to Watton Hall."

Her brother nodded solemnly.

"I did. I am sorry, Charlotte. I had to. I had to warn him."

"Warn him about me?"

He sat beside her.

"Charlotte, please understand, when James came back, he was different. He had suffered so much and seen so many terrible things. You saw how Father reacted - do you think James met anything different elsewhere? He could hardly bear to look at himself. I can only imagine what it was for him to be looked on in such a manner by others."

Charlotte lowered her gaze as she considered the hurt that James must have felt to be treated in such a manner, just because of his face.

"Why did you not tell me he was alive?"

"Because it would have made no difference," William answered. "By the time I knew James had returned, you were already betrothed to Malcolm. James knew this and wanted you to pursue the match. He did not want his presence to cause any interference, and asked me to keep his return a secret."

"From me?" Charlotte exclaimed.

"Yes, from you. Charlotte, we both know that you would not have married Malcolm if you knew that James was alive. He did not want that for you. He knew you were happy and that was enough for him. He wanted to live a quiet, reclusive life. How could I deny him that, after everything? I kept my word."

"You should have told me."

"I am sorry, Charlotte. I hope that you can forgive me. I only wanted to do what was best for everyone. You seemed happy in your match with Malcolm. It allowed you to leave our father's house and find your own way, to make your home as you wanted it, and James could live in peace as he wished. I saw no harm in it. You were both happy. I never imagined that you would have any reason to return to this county, or that James' secret would be revealed."

"But it has been revealed," Charlotte answered, "and that has changed everything."

"I imagine it has," William agreed. "I hope it has not changed things between us," he added. "I do not want there to be any issues between us, Charlotte."

She smiled at her brother gently.

"I think I understand why you did what you did. However, I cannot forgive you."

"Charlotte."

She raised a hand to silence him.

"Hear me out. I will not forgive you unless you agree to help me."

Her brother frowned.

"Help you? Help you do what?"

"I want to find out the truth. You must help me to see James again."

"Charlotte, he does not want it," William protested.

"That does not matter. I *must* see him. I must settle the matter between us." She looked at her brother intently. "I must have peace on this."

CHAPTER SEVEN

A week later

He heard the sound of the carriage approaching, and his heart thudded at the prospect that it might be Charlotte. He peered through the window as it stopped outside the door, and relief filled him when he saw that it was William who stepped down from it. But with the relief, there was also disappointment.

James left the library, intent on meeting his friend near the door, but he stopped when he heard William and his father in conversation. He stayed hidden as he listened, for he was the topic of their conversation.

"Mr. Watts," William's greeting was cheerful.

"William, how good to see you, young man. Or should I say, Lord Cott?"

His father took his friend's hand and shook it vigorously.

"We are of too close acquaintance for such formalities," William replied. "William will do very well."

"If you will have me forget formality when addressing you, then I insist you do the same with me. You are a man now - surely calling me by my forename cannot be an offense to either of us?"

William laughed lightly.

"Agreed, thank you, John."

James' father cleared his throat.

"What brings you here today?"

"I know that Charlotte has learned the truth and that she has been here frequently in the hope of seeing James again, but has not been received. I came to see James about it."

His jaw clenched as he listened. William was there to discuss Charlotte. It was one conversation he most definitely did not wish to have, for he was doing his best to try to forget her, but it was futile. He did not need her brother to further remind him.

"I am glad you have come," his father replied. "I have been very concerned about my son. Perhaps you can help me?"

"I will do anything I can," William replied as the pair started to walk. James used a tapestry to further conceal himself. "I have not seen James so disheartened since his return," his father stated. "He locks himself away, even from us. I have tried to speak to him but he will not hear me. I am afraid he might do himself harm."

"Truly?" William questioned.

James was appalled. He was many things, but suicidal was not one of them.

"I do. I have done all I can, but my son will not acknowledge my words. I also have Beatrice to think of. She is as concerned for him as I am. She also wonders why Lady Charlotte stays away and I have to find excuses for it."

"You have not told her?"

"How can I?" his father replied. "And upset her further. No, I have decided she should believe that busyness with her affairs keeps Lady Charlotte away, and I assure her that she will visit as soon as she can. I cannot risk Beatrice's health with the truth. I asked Lady Charlotte to visit us again, but her refusal to do so, I believe, is due to James' request."

"I understand. Charlotte would want to avoid further contention between them, for she hopes some middle ground can be found. She would not want to upset any chance of that." William sighed. "I will do whatever I can do to bring peace to your home once more," William assured Mr. Watts. "You have my word."

"And what precisely will you do?" James interrupted, stepping into view, unable to listen further and not speak. He felt guilty as it was, but to listen to his father only made that guilt worse.

"James."

He walked toward them and bowed his head politely.

"Father. William."

His father looked between them hesitantly.

"I think it best that I excuse myself and allow you to talk to each other. I will be in your stepmother's room if you need me."

James watched as his father removed himself from

the scene and quickly walked up the stairs to be with his stepmother.

"So, you have come to scold me?" he said before turning back to his friend. "Or have you come to 'help' me?"

He met William's eye and waited for an answer.

"I have not come to scold, but I would help in any way if I only could," William answered.

James nodded.

"Then we'd best speak elsewhere. Follow me. I get enough stares without creating servants' gossip to add to it."

William agreed and followed him to the library. Once inside, they sat opposite each other in the big wing-back chairs.

"I am frightfully sorry I did not come sooner," William began. "Things have been very busy on the estate, and father has had me at his side constantly."

"And your sister, of course," James added.

"Yes, Charlotte and George keep me busy as well, but it does not mean that I have not wanted to be here. I cannot imagine what you must be going through at this time."

"I would rather talk of something else," James admitted.

William looked at him sympathetically.

"I am afraid there is not much else to speak of, James. I could ask you how you spend your days, but I already know you have been reading and brooding. I believe the latter more than the former."

James chuckled bitterly.

"You know me too well, my friend."

"It is because I am a friend that I am here," William replied. "I am worried about you and Charlotte."

"What is the matter with Lady Benton?" He used her formal title in the hope it might give him some distance from the girl he'd loved, but it did little to salve his pain.

"James, what do you think? She worries about you. She is determined to find out the truth, or whatever it is that she is seeking. You know her. She is relentless, sometimes to the detriment of her own well-being. Much as she would hate me saying it, that trait is one she inherited from our father."

James stood and strode to the window.

"I know your sister. Lady Benton has always been very determined. I thought that what I said would dissuade her. I thought that if I pushed hard enough..."

"That she would run away?" William laughed. "James, you of all people, should know it takes much more than that to make Charlotte turn from what she has set her mind on. Especially as it pertains to you. How many times did she defy father to be with you? And that was in our youth. Now she is a woman with a mind of her own."

James folded his fist and pressed it to the frame of the window by his head.

"I know. Still, I thought what I said was sufficiently harsh to make her want to forget about me."

He could hear William sigh behind him.

"The best times of our lives have involved you, James. How could you expect Charlotte to forget that? How could she forget the love she had for you? The love she still seems to have for you. Will you not see her?"

James turned immediately.

"I cannot! You know that!"

"James, she has missed you. We all do. Why not take this turn of events as an opportunity?"

"An opportunity for what?"

"To restore our friendships to what they once were. We had such a wonderful kinship," William answered as he got to his feet. He walked toward him. "I miss it. I am sure you miss us too."

"What if I do?" James replied. "What good would come of it?"

"All the good in the world. James, we can once again be as we were. You would no longer have to be alone. You would not have to fear the comments and looks of others. Charlotte does not care about your scars. Nor do I, and Charlotte has done nothing but think of your feelings, and not your appearance."

His words struck James. It was a wonderful concept, but one he did not think as easily achieved as William believed. Still, he could not deny the appeal of having his dearest friends once more in his acquaintance, openly. Dinners and walks by the lake came to mind and other things they had once done, like...

"Fishing," he commented absently as a smile spread across his face.

"Yes," William agreed. "You remember those times? How good they were? They can be that good again if you will only allow it."

His words tugged at James. He wanted it to be true,

to be that simple, but nothing in the world was that way any longer, at least not for him.

"William, I cannot..."

"Why not? What have you to lose? You have spent the past few years hiding away in this house, living a half-life so that Charlotte could be happy. And she no longer is. She is unhappy and made all the unhappier because you will not see her. You did this for her, my friend, and yet you are now both unhappy. Is it not better to end this terrible misunderstanding and tell her your true feelings?" James' eyes rushed to meet William's. His friend smiled at him. "What? Do you think I do not know why you do these things? Why you try to push Charlotte away? Do you think I do not know that you still love my sister? That you always have?" James was momentarily dumbstruck. "Come, friend. Let us be honest with one another. You love my sister," William reiterated.

James swallowed his pride and fear to answer him.

"William, it is as you just said, I have always loved her. You know that. But it is because I cannot love her that I do this."

"Who says that you cannot?"

"The whole world," James replied. He sighed. *I do.*

William laid a hand on his shoulder.

"And since when have we cared about the whole world? We have cared for each other, defying even my father to do as we three wished. Why can it not be that way again?"

"William."

"James, I think it is time you told Charlotte the truth.

I think you should tell her how you truly feel. We will all be the better for it."

James stared at his friend, but could not speak. Would it indeed be better?

"How could I ever make up for what I said to her?" He shook his head. "No, I cannot. Lady Benton may be unhappy now, but she would be even more unhappy if she were with me."

"You cannot make these decisions for her," William challenged. "No one has ever decided what Charlotte felt, but Charlotte. Please, give her a chance? Give yourselves a chance."

CHAPTER EIGHT

S he could not keep still as she waited for William's return. Her brother had promised to help her, and she was sure he would keep his word. Still, anxiety gnawed at her. Could William persuade James to see her? They remained close and William had kept his secret for so long, perhaps the bond between them had not diminished as had the connection between herself and James.

"You will wear a hole in the floor," her father warned. He peered over the top of his newspaper to look at her. "Would you sit down? You are bound to make yourself sick."

"I will be fine," Charlotte assured him. She wrung her hands anxiously, her teeth taking hold of her bottom lip. "What could be taking William so long?"

The sound of the closing of the newspaper got her attention. Her father was annoyed and folded the periodical neatly and slapped it against his leg.

"It seems I am to have no peace, even in my own

parlor." He stood. "If it suits you, I shall withdraw to my study. I should be able to have some quiet there."

Charlotte took a deep breath and bowed her head politely.

"Yes, Father. I am sorry for disturbing you."

"As you should be." His frank gaze settled on her. "Since your return, you have managed to cause disquiet in my home such as I have never known it before. I do hope you will consider the honor of this house and this family before you venture to cause more disturbances."

Charlotte lowered her eyes from his disappointed gaze.

"Of course, Father."

She did not lift them until he was out of the room.

She was torn by her emotions. She was half hope and half fear at what news her brother would have to give her when he returned. No one understood what she felt. No one could ever understand how her heart had broken on the day she was told of James' death. It was as if her own life had come to an end, yet she continued to live, pointlessly.

Tears stung her eyes as she remembered that fateful day. The look on her father and brother's faces as Mr Watts and Mrs Watts had come to inform them of their loss. It was a waking nightmare, one Charlotte had been forced to live with, for all of these years. Now, she could awake from it. She could not undo what was done, but she could start anew. They all could. If only James would let her get close.

Did he feel not the same? The story he'd told her, of no longer wanting her, did not ring true in her spirit.

There was something more to it. There simply had to be. Charlotte was aware that it might be her foolish hope which refused to let go of her former desires, but whatever it was, she had to know the truth if there was any hope of her living out the rest of her life in peace.

The sound of thunder startled her. Charlotte glanced out the window. She had not noticed the turn in the weather, but the fork of lightning that danced across the sky told her a storm was brewing. A thunderstorm.

"I hope William returns before the storm breaks."

She turned to her seat and settled upon it. Her embroidery sat on the chaise nearby, but Charlotte did not even consider it. Her ears were pricked for the sound of William's carriage, her thoughts her only company. Charlotte closed her eyes and the image of James appeared before her. His scarred face brought pain to her heart. What had happened to him? How had he survived such a heinous injury?

She wondered aloud. "What did it do to him?"

She knew nothing of war and was glad of that. Men's willingness to slaughter each other for one purpose or another was something Charlotte could never understand. She had learned the precious value of life, being raised without a mother, but the awful pain of it was brought fully to her for the first time with James' believed passing. It was only then that it became real.

I pray that George never knows of it either.

Charlotte got to her feet, no longer able to sit still. Where was William? She went to the window, just as another flash of lightning illuminated the ground enough for her to see the carriage approaching.

"He's here!"

Charlotte ran from the room, her father's words forgotten as she passed the household staff in a rush. She was panting when she reached the front door. William rushed into the entrance hall dripping wet, his coat and hat were soaked through, even from the short distance from the carriage to the house.

"Mrs. Churchill" he cried. "Prepare a guest room and call the physician."

Her brother's urgent cry forced Charlotte to stop.

"What has happened?"

Her brother turned to her but had no chance to respond as the coachman came in moments later with what appeared to be a large bundle of wet clothing in his arms. It took Charlotte a moment to realize that the misshapen form was that of a young woman. Her eyes widened in surprise.

"What is this? Who is she?"

William took the young woman from the coachman and cradled her against his body. He rushed toward the stairs.

"I do not know. We came upon her on the edge of the road some miles away. I almost missed her in the dark, but a fortuitous flash of lightning allowed me to glimpse her."

Charlotte followed close behind him.

"What on earth would she be doing on the road alone? Are you sure that there was no one with her?"

"I tried to discern that from her, but she was barely conscious. As soon as I lifted her into the carriage, she fell into unconsciousness, and I have not been able to rouse her since. Who knows how long she was out there?"

"Or what might have happened to her if you had not come along."

Her brother glanced at her over his shoulder.

"I dread the thought."

The maids were preparing the room as William rushed inside. The lamps were lit, the bed curtains pulled back and the sheets pulled down. William laid the young woman in the midst of it as the maids set about building up a fire in the grate.

Charlotte came to his side immediately, her hand moving to the young woman's forehead.

"She is burning up with fever. Get blankets and towels," she told one maid. "Get a night rail from my rooms," she instructed another. "Her clothing is soaked through."

Both women ran to fulfill her commands.

William stepped back. He was still soaking wet.

"You will be no better than her if you stay in those clothes." She took him by the arm. "I insist you get out of them this instant."

"I cannot help it, Charlotte. I have never seen so pitiful a creature in all my life," William commented. His eyes were still fixed on the small frame beneath the mountain of bedcoverings.

Charlotte glanced at the young woman. Her skin was pale and her cheeks gaunt. Dark circles surrounded her eyes and her hair was too wet for Charlotte to be sure of its color.

"I must say, I agree with you."

"Perhaps I should go for the physician," he suggested.

Charlotte turned at his words.

"You most certainly will not. I saw one of the footmen set off to fetch him, as soon as you had said the words when you entered the house." Charlotte led her brother from the room. It was just like him to show such concern for a stranger. The poor girl was in a terrible state. "I hope that Doctor Mortimer will be here soon."

William nodded.

Charlotte accompanied her brother to his room where she left him, firmly telling his valet to assist him to change immediately. She returned to the young woman's bedchamber to sit with her until the doctor arrived.

Her initial opinion of the young woman's condition worsened as the layers of wet material were removed from her body. She was little more than skin and bones. The sight of her was distressing.

Charlotte watched as the maids changed the young woman's clothing, slipping her into one of Charlotte's warm winter night rails, and setting her own worn clothing aside to dry near the fire.

"Who could have done such a thing as to allow her to end up in a storm, in this condition?"

Her brother stepped back into the room at that point, wearing dry, but obviously very hastily donned clothing. He ignored Charlotte's question. Charlotte regarded his rather rumpled appearance with a raised eyebrow.

"I will be well, Charlotte – I do not need to look elegant at this moment. It is she I am concerned about - she does not look good."

The maids shook their heads but did not comment. It

was obvious they agreed. The unanswered question still hung in the room, uppermost in everyone's minds - what deplorable conditions had that poor girl escaped from?

Doctor Mortimer arrived almost an hour later. By that time the fire was roaring in the young woman's bedchamber and she was covered with every spare blanket they had to offer. Her father was less than impressed by the use of his good bed linens when he stepped into the room with the doctor.

Ignoring the doctor's request that he leave the room – a request which William reluctantly complied with – her father launched into complaint.

"On an urchin?" he protested. "Charlotte, have you gone mad?"

"No, Father," she replied, forcing herself to hold her tongue, to be calm in her response. "The young woman needs our care. You would not want it known that a poor girl came to this house for aid and died from cold because you would not allow her the use of your linens."

Her father was silent.

"You could have used the blankets from the stables."

Charlotte looked at him incredulously.

"But those are for the horses!"

Her father's face contorted in displeasure as he raised a finger to his nose.

"She smells like one."

The young woman did, indeed, have an odor about her, but Charlotte was sure it was the smell of the road on her and not the young woman herself. Her hair was caked with mud and debris from the field. There was no telling what may have befallen her or into what terrible mud puddles she may have fallen.

"Father, where is your compassion? How can you be so blind to her state?"

Her father looked at her pointedly.

"I am very aware and have the utmost compassion. I give charity regularly, as you know."

"But you prefer your charity to end there, and not have it on your doorstep?" Charlotte retorted.

Her father was ambivalent.

"I was not made for such things."

"Then leave it to me. I will care for our guest and when she is well, she will be gone from this house at no more expense to you than a child," Charlotte replied. "I only ask that you do not distress her while she is here. It is clear she has been through a terrible ordeal."

Charlotte looked at the young woman with pity. She could not imagine being treated in such a manner, that one would end up so gaunt and abandoned in a storm, or what circumstances might have brought her to such a state.

I only hope we can help her.

Doctor Mortimer stepped forward, and Charlotte could see that he was exasperated.

"If you do not mind, I need to examine the patient. Please leave this room."

"Yes, of course, Doctor, though I must insist that Mrs Churchill remain as a chaperone."

Doctor Mortimer nodded and began to examine his patient.

Relieved that her father had so easily acquiesced to

the request, Charlotte left the room after him. He returned to the solitude of his study, while she sought out William. Doctor Mortimer would do his best for the girl, she was confident of that – but there were things Charlotte needed to know now.

She found her brother sipping a cup of hot tea with whiskey by the fire in the parlor. The words which followed came unceremoniously.

"Did you see him? Did you see James?" She stepped closer to him, eagerness propelling her forward. She repeated her question. "Did you see him?"

William took a visible breath.

"I did."

"And?"

"We spoke. However, I think that, for now, time is needed. You have both gone through so much. This should not be rushed."

"But William..."

"Charlotte, trust me. I know whereof I speak. I believe it is best that, for the moment, you allow James time to think, to gather his thoughts, and then see if his mind has altered from its previous position."

Her brother's words were disappointing - she had hoped he would have changed James' mind immediately. She should have known that such a thing was near impossible. It was too soon. In some things, James had always been as capable of stubbornness as she was herself.

"I suppose I should not have expected a miracle," she replied. Her voice was sad, even to her own ears. "I just hoped... that is... I so wanted for us to be as we were." She raised her eyes to her brother. "The way we were."

William reached for her hand.

"I want this as well. That is why I caution you to give James time, Charlotte. Give yourself some time."

Her eyebrows raised at his words.

"Me? Why would I need time?"

"Because you have had a shock, my dear. After all, the love of your life has just seemingly risen as from the dead. It is a great deal for the mind and heart to take," William replied calmly. He smiled at her. "And I can tell your heart is still very much invested in the resolution of this situation."

Charlotte wanted to reply - but what could she say? Her brother was right. She lowered her eyes from his gaze.

"You know me far too well, Brother."

"One would hope so, after all these many years," he mused.

Charlotte smiled back.

"All right," she said quietly. "I shall do as you ask. I will focus my energy on helping that poor soul in our guest room, and on my own feelings. Perhaps I need to search my soul and see whether my feelings are selfish or selfless?"

"You are not a selfish person, Charlotte," William replied firmly. "However, you can be rather singularly focused at times."

He laughed slightly and she laughed with him.

"You put it mildly, brother."

William nodded.

"What are brothers for?" He sipped his toddy. "Where is our father?"

"I am afraid that I have made Father rather cross this evening," Charlotte confessed. "I questioned his morals."

William shook his head, smiling.

"I will be sure to avoid him in that case."

The topic of James was dropped thereafter, at least in their conversation. Naturally, Charlotte still had questions but she refrained from asking them. William thought she needed time, and so did James. She would do as he asked. She would give him the time he needed.

Not too much, I hope. I do not think I could go forever without knowing the truth.

CHAPTER NINE

Two weeks later

The sound of coughing filled her ears, as concern wrinkled Charlotte's brow. She dropped the cloth into the basin of water and, after soaking it, wrung it out and placed it on the young woman's forehead.

The fever persisted, but Doctor Mortimer assured her it would break in a few days. The young woman was improving gradually, but the process was slow. Still, Charlotte worried for her.

She had hardly eaten since she'd arrived in their home, and she was already so frail and fragile that Charlotte feared the effects of the fever and illness would only worsen her already birdlike condition.

Charlotte traced a gentle finger along her charge's brow. The girl was like a helpless child, and Charlotte felt much as she would have if she had been caring for

George. However, it was more than the maternal instinct which drove her. Calamity had befallen the young woman, the same as it had many others, every day. Charlotte should, she supposed, be inured to it, as the way of the world – but she was not – not, at least, when the sufferer of calamity came to her direct attention, as this girl had. Her condition moved Charlotte to an aching sympathy.

"You must get better. You must tell us who you are."

Charlotte did not know if the young woman could hear her, but it did not stop her from regularly uttering encouragement. She was once again passing the cloth over the young woman's brow when the girl's lips opened, and she murmured something. Charlotte stopped immediately, unsure if she had heard correctly, or if it had simply been a sigh or a moan. The young woman murmured again, and this time Charlotte was certain she was hearing a tangle of words.

She leaned closer, straining to hear.

"What did you say?" The voice that spoke was soft and a little hoarse. No doubt, a parched throat from fever was to blame, despite Charlotte's repeated spooning of water between her lips over the last few days. "Say it again? I cannot understand."

The woman in the bed spoke again, this time louder.

"Mary."

Charlotte's brow smoothed and a small smile lifted her cheeks.

"Mary? Is that your name?"

A weak nod answered her.

Charlotte's smile broadened.

"Good day to you, Mary. My name is Charlotte. You are at Caldor House near Alnerton Village, and you are safe."

Her words went unanswered, as deeper, slower breaths indicated that Mary had fallen into sleep again.

Charlotte smiled - finally, they had a name to call her. She would tell William when he came out of his study. Her brother had defied their father, almost shockingly, and insisted that he could as easily check the ledgers from Caldor House as anywhere, and had barely left the house since bringing home their young patient.

She continued her caretaking, moistening Mary's face and neck with cool water to help lower her fever. It was slowly declining, and the fact that she had spoken, for the first time since her arrival, meant that she was indeed improving. Knowing there was progress comforted Charlotte.

Charlotte remained by Mary's side until the water had lost all its coolness, and Mary's face was, for the first time, close to a normal temperature. Then she dropped the cloth back into the bowl and left the room, calling for one of the maids to collect the bowl and refill it with fresh, cool water, and then stay with Mary for a while. Once that was arranged, Charlotte stood in the upstairs hall and stretched to relieve the ache in her back. Bending over for so long took a toll after a while and she was feeling aches and pains everywhere.

She had intended to check George, before returning to Mary's side, but, as she straightened from her stretching, she was met by the sight of her brother approaching.

"William, are you finished with the ledgers already?"

"Not quite. But I wanted to check on her. How is she today?"

Charlotte smiled, pleased to have good news to share.

"She spoke today, just one word, but an important one. She told me her name. She is called Mary."

William smiled.

"Mary. Nothing more? She did not give her surname? Perhaps we might find out more about her if we knew that."

Charlotte shook her head.

"Just the one name - that was all she said before she fell back into a healing sleep – but her fever has eased - perhaps later, or tomorrow, she will have the strength to tell us more."

JAMES PACED THE ROOM ANXIOUSLY. He counted the strides, his ears strained for the sound of anyone approaching from the outside. His brow was furrowed with consternation. Charlotte no longer came to the house, and what was worse, neither did William. Their absence caused disquiet in his spirit.

"Something must have happened," he said to no one. James stalked to the window and looked out. There was no one there. "Something is simply not right."

He knew Charlotte. She would never give up so easily. Something must have happened to stop her from coming. Despite his claims to want her gone, James still enjoyed the sight of Charlotte every time she defied him.

It was a torturous pleasure, but it warmed his heart. He had to find out what had happened.

James usually avoided the household staff but today he would go against his practice to get news of Charlotte and her family. He marched from his room in search of one of the maids.

"Betsy? Betsy, a word?"

The young woman looked at him in bewilderment. He'd never spoken a word to her since her arrival several months before. *She must wonder what I want with her*, he thought.

She bowed her head slightly.

"Yes, Captain?"

"Have you heard of any goings-on at Caldor House?"

The young woman's eyes shifted in her head. Her lips tightened slightly.

"Betsy?"

"Yes, sir. I'd not like to involve myself in gossip, sir, but I did hear that there is some illness there. I heard one of the scullery maids saying that Doctor Mortimer advised no one to visit the house as there was the young lady there, who possibly has a contagious fever."

James's heart began to pound against his ribs.

"What?"

"Yes, Captain. That is what I heard. No one has been there since Lord Cott last came to visit this house.

"Did you hear anything else?" James questioned. "Was there any word of what sort of contagion? Or of what caused it? Or whom it has afflicted?"

The maid shook her head. "No, sir. Nothing like that was talked about. May I go now? I have my chores.."

James barely registered her words but dismissed her with a wave of his hand. His heart was beating too loudly to hear much else. The young lady of the house was ill. He whispered her name as fear began to creep into his chest.

"Charlotte."

James no longer hesitated. The sound of her name on his lips brought him to life. He ran to his father's office and rushed in unannounced.

"Father, have you heard of the illness at Caldor House?"

John Watts looked up at him from his work.

"James, what brings you to my office in such a state?"

James repeated his question.

"The illness at Caldor House. Have you heard anything of it?" He stepped behind a chair and gripped it for balance. Terrible thoughts were running through his head and the racing of his heart threatened his ability to remain composed.

"I have," his father answered. "What of it?"

"What of it?" James repeated. "Father, Charlotte and William are there. How could you know this and say nothing to me?"

His father looked at him frankly.

"I did not think that you cared. Were you not the one who forbade her from this house and refused to see her? Are you not also the same man who told her you wanted her out of his life? Why should I think you should care if illness came to her house?"

James stood in disbelief.

"Yes, I said those things but you know I did not mean them."

"Did you not?" his father questioned. He shrugged. "I did not think you did. Yet you seemed quite adamant that it was the only way to proceed." He held James' gaze. "There was no other choice. Those were your words."

James' draw dropped.

"Father, you cannot be serious."

"James, if you care for Lady Charlotte then you do not need me to be your go-between. If you were truly interested in her well-being you would go and find out for yourself. Otherwise, leave her alone."

He stared at his father blankly, but his father spoke no more. Instead, he turned his eyes back to his work and left James a silent observer.

"Father."

"You heard me, James. If you want to know about Lady Charlotte's health, you will have to find the answer for yourself." He smiled slightly. "I believe you know how that is done."

How could his father do this to him? Surely, he knew there was no way Charlotte could be ill, or in danger, and not have him respond? Why didn't he just tell him?

You know why. Because he wants you to do it yourself. He's forcing you to see her.

James turned from the room.

If Charlotte were ill, there was no way he could remain at home, as if nothing had happened. He momentarily considered asking the rest of the staff, but the looks he got as he passed them in the hallway quickly changed his mind. He dared not ask them, knowing how fearful the servant class was of infection. He would not subject himself to their stares. There was only one choice left.

"Mrs. Boyle?"

He called the woman's name as he approached her. Unlike the others, she did not react negatively to the sight of him.

"Yes, Master James. How may I help?"

He hesitated to speak. The words were heavy on his tongue. Finally, he forced them out.

"Please send to the stables and have them prepare the carriage for me. I am going out."

A smile began to spread across the housekeeper's face.

"Very well, Master James. I shall have the coachman ready the carriage. How soon do you wish to leave?"

James smiled slightly at the fact that his request had not been met by surprise, as he'd expected it to be.

"As soon as possible, please Mrs. Boyle."

Mrs. Boyle nodded her head.

"I will see to it straight away. How far will you be traveling? Should I have a hot brick put inside ready?"

"No need, Mrs. Boyle. I am only going as far as Caldor House."

Again, James saw a smile tug at the housekeeper's lips.

"I shall notify you immediately when the carriage is ready."

Mrs. Boyle walked away as James' heart began to pound. *Was he going to do this? Was he going to leave this house?*

Yes, you are. You know that you are. The only way to

find out the truth is to find out for yourself. You don't have to stay long. Just long enough to see if Charlotte is well. Once you are sure of it, you can leave. It is that simple.

James tried to reassure himself as he went upstairs to retrieve his coat and hat. As he came back down, he could hear the crunch of the carriage wheels on the gravel outside the house and waved Mrs. Boyle off as she appeared.

"I heard it arrive – thank you."

The housekeeper smiled, and he stepped through the front door, seeing the carriage waiting for him at the bottom of the steps.

He did not look at the coachman as he entered the carriage, but he could feel his gaze upon him. James steeled himself. He would receive more stares when he arrived at Caldor House, no doubt. It was best to mentally prepare himself now.

James's heart thumped harshly in his chest. What if something were wrong with Charlotte? What if she is gravely ill? The thought was abhorrent to him. A world in which Charlotte did not exist, was no world at all. He took a deep breath to calm himself. *She must be well.*

"Coachman, stop!"

The tightness in his chest was almost unbearable. He needed to catch his breath.

The carriage stopped and before the coachman could step down from the box, James was already out, standing on the side of the road. He began to walk back and forth, his hands on his hips as he took long breaths.

Get a grip on yourself, James. You are better than this. Do not let a small visit such as this undo you. You fought in the war - visiting Caldor House is nothing in comparison.

"Are you quite well, Captain?" the coachman called to him.

James raised a hand to him and lied.

"Perfectly. I had a cramp in my calf and needed to stretch it out." He flexed his leg exaggeratedly. "It seems to be alright now. Shall we continue?"

He walked back to the carriage and swung up in, not bothering to let down the steps, and pulled the door closed after him as he settled onto the seat.

They arrived at Caldor House far sooner than he'd thought they would - either the coachman had driven the horses faster than usual, or his fears had made the journey seem short to him. Regardless of the reason, he looked up at the intimidating structure and took a deep breath as he stepped out of the carriage.

"Wait for me. I shall not be long," he instructed the coachman.

The man nodded.

"Yes, Captain."

His chest felt tight as he climbed the front steps, but James refused to be stopped by it. He took hold of the large brass knocker and brought it down three times against the door. There was a time when he had not needed to knock at this house, for the household staff had known to expect him at the same time every day.

But that was a lifetime ago.

He waited for someone to answer.

Mrs Churchill appeared at the door moments later.

The shock at seeing him was evident in her expression. Her jaw slackened and her eyes grew large.

"Is Lady Benton at home?"

Mrs Churchill nodded.

"Yes, Captain Watts, shall I announce you?"

He felt a small pang of comfort that she was there and able to accept visitors. Perhaps his fears were unwarranted.

You have to be sure.

James swallowed the lump in his throat.

He nodded politely.

"Yes."

"I see. Please follow me, Captain."

James followed her through the familiar corridors. The same paintings still hung on the walls. The wallpapers were the same, as were the furnishings - the Duke of Mormont was not a man who favored change. James knew Caldor House as well as he knew his own home. There wasn't a nook or cranny he had not explored or hidden in, at one stage or another. It had been a second home to him in years past.

Stares and whispers followed them as they passed other members of the household staff in the corridors. James had expected his appearance would cause a disturbance among them and he had not been wrong in that belief. The last time he had visited the house it had been the same. He steeled himself and kept his head high, pretending not to notice their reactions.

They were almost to the parlor, and James was thankful for it when the sound of his name rang out through the house.

"James!"

The housekeeper stopped before him, forcing him to pause as well. He looked up and saw Charlotte and William on the balcony above him.

James was speechless. Charlotte looked remarkably well. Her dark hair was pulled into a fetching bun atop her head, her curls framing her angelic face as she looked at him with large, cheerful eyes. He couldn't breathe. The sight of her had utterly stolen the breath from his lungs.

CHAPTER TEN

W illiam offered her his arm.
" Where were you going? I will accompany
you."

"I was just going to check on George, and to stretch
my legs," Charlotte answered. As they began to walk
along the hallway, she glanced down over the balcony rail
towards the front door, expecting to see nothing more
than a bored footman, or other staff, going about their
work. But the sight that met her shocked her into stillness
as her heart faltered, her breath hitched and her pulse
raced.

James was there, standing beside Mrs. Churchill. It
hardly seemed real.

The moment Charlotte saw him, standing in her
father's house, she lost all sense of reason. She was so
shocked that his name leaped from her lips unbidden.
She immediately reprimanded herself, as her brother's
gaze settled on her. He knew, as well as she did, that their
father would not be pleased with such an outburst.

William escorted her down the stairs to where James stood. He smiled at his friend and welcomed him.

"James, what a surprise to see you. I am happy you have decided to call on us."

William looked at Charlotte, but she could find no words for what felt like an eternity. Finally, she found her voice.

"What brings you here?"

James' gaze shifted between her and William.

"I heard there was illness in the house. I feared that you were ill."

Charlotte frowned, but it soon melted into a smile.

He cares.

"I am sorry, but you were misinformed. I am very well. There is, however, a young woman here, whom Doctor Mortimer is treating. She is recovering slowly."

"A young woman?" James questioned. "Is she some relation?"

"No," William answered. "It was a chance encounter. I found her on the side of the road between Watton Hall and Caldor House, in the middle of the storm that broke out as I returned from speaking with you. I brought her here, near death from the cold and seeming privation. She has been under Doctor Mortimer's care ever since. Her name is Mary, but we know little more about her than that."

James' eyes lowered momentarily.

"I see. The poor girl."

When they rose again it was to meet hers. Charlotte's breath caught in her lungs. The sad discomfort in his eyes tore at her.

"Since you are here, perhaps this is a good opportunity for the two of you to speak?" William looked between them. "I think it would be a mistake not to take it." He smiled. "If you will both excuse me, I have some more ledgers to attend to. I'll summon your companion, Miss Lefebvre for you."

Charlotte and James were silent as William excused himself. They looked at each other, and uncertainty filled the air between them. Would he stay or leave? She decided to try to keep him with her, at least for a little while.

"Would you walk with me?" James looked hesitant. "Just a short walk. I promise I won't keep you long."

Charlotte hoped her encouragement would persuade him that she just wanted to talk to him. That was all – at least, that was what she told herself, but inside, she knew she wanted far more.

"I can only stay a short while," James finally answered. "The carriage is waiting for me."

Charlotte suppressed the joy that filled her. She nodded quickly. "Very well, just a short while. Not long."

They lingered in the corridor until Sophie joined them. The young woman, who had become Charlotte's companion before her marriage, had remained with her through the years. Even though she had no longer truly needed a companion as a married woman, Sophie had become a friend and she had not wanted to be parted from her. After Malcolm's death, Sophie had become the rock she clung to, to cope, at least at first.

"Madame," Sophie greeted her, then she turned to James and curtseyed. "Monsieur."

James bowed.

"James, may I present Miss Sophie Lefebvre. Sophie, may I present Captain James Watts."

Sophie's eyes became like saucers. She looked at James.

"Captain Watts?"

"Yes? Are we acquainted?" James questioned.

"No, Monsieur. It is just that I have heard of you. It is a pleasure to have this opportunity to meet you."

James nodded.

"The pleasure is all mine, Miss Lefebvre."

"Shall we go to the garden?"

Charlotte waited for the acknowledgment of her question, suddenly afraid he would not stay. But James nodded, and the trio walked from the corridor to the rear of the house. Sophie walked somewhat behind them, granting them some illusion of privacy. Charlotte almost laughed – as a widow, she did not truly need a chaperone, but her father's rather inflated sense of importance insisted on the utmost propriety, and poor Sophie was, thereby, expected to trail after Charlotte at times.

The sun was hidden by clouds as they walked into the garden. The fresh air was invigorating, after being inside for so long. She'd spent most of her days looking after Mary and had barely stepped outside.

"The weather has been fine in recent days."

James nodded.

"Yes. Quite fine. The gardens look well-kept."

"Father takes great care to ensure that they are," Charlotte commented.

The corners of James' lips rose slightly to hide a smile.

"Yes, he does take great pains to ensure that everything is perfect."

Charlotte smiled.

"That he does."

They walked for several minutes more in silence. James' arms were folded behind his back, and his head held high, almost stiffly. Charlotte couldn't help but glance in his direction whenever she got the opportunity.

Though the scars marred his face, they did not detract from his attractiveness, at least to her. The contours were still the same, his eyes were still the portals to his thoughts, which she could read so easily.

"I did not think you would ever come to see me," she admitted.

James turned to her.

"In truth, I had not intended to. But when I heard of an illness at Caldor House, I presumed it was you and came to enquire after your health."

Charlotte smiled.

"I did not think you cared. Was that not what you said at our last meeting?"

James bowed his head, his eyes fixing on the gravel of the path.

"I said a great deal at our last meeting." He lifted his eyes to her. "I suppose my presence here gives away the truth of my feelings."

"It does. Though I did not believe what you said that day, in the first place," Charlotte admitted. "Your eyes never lie, even when your lips do."

James smiled slightly.

"You are not easy to deceive, Lady Benton." She raised her eyebrows quizzically at his use of her title. He gave a rueful grin.

"I never have been," she said. "Though I will give you this, for a moment, I wondered. Then, I thought about it and knew it could not be true. Your words were convincing, but then when I thought of your eyes and of everything we have been through, I could not believe them."

James changed the subject.

"The young woman, Mary. How is she?"

"She is faring better. I still worry, but she seems to be on the road to recovery. She is still very weak - if you could have seen her, James, she was no more than skin and bones when William brought her home. She can only speak a little but has so far refused to answer any questions apart from her name. I fear she has suffered some terrible ordeal."

"It is good that William found her when he did. I can think of no two better people to look after her."

Charlotte smiled at James' confidence in them.

"Thank you. We are doing our best, given the circumstances. Father, as you might expect, is not happy with the situation of having a possible ne'er-do-well under his roof."

"Your father," James commented. "He is always apt to think the worst before giving any person the benefit of the doubt."

"It is something we have long accepted about him. Though at times I still marvel at how callous he can be to the plight of others." Charlotte met James' eye. "Such as yours."

James stopped walking immediately. He looked at her in silence for a long moment.

"I had best go."

That said, he went to turn away, back towards the house, to leave, but Charlotte reached for his hand.

"Please, not yet. I am sorry. Perhaps I should not have said that."

"You always say just what is on your mind."

"Maybe I should learn to curtail that," Charlotte commented. Her eyes turned to Sophie, who was watching them intently. She released James's hand. "Please stay. I just want to talk. It has been so long since we have talked. Do you not miss it?"

James took a visible deep breath. "What do you want to talk about?"

Charlotte couldn't believe her ears. Would he answer her questions? Could she be so lucky as to obtain that from him this easily?

"I want the truth. I want to know what happened to you."

James held her gaze for a long time.

"You might not want to hear it."

"You have never said anything that I did not want to hear – well apart from your untrue words at our last meeting." Charlotte smiled at him. "You never will."

"Then we had best walk. The fresh air might make this easier," James replied. He started to walk again.

Charlotte walked beside him, her steps matching his. He was dressed well, as always. His dark attire suited him but gave his pale skin an even paler hue. He used to have more color to him, she thought – of a certainty, it was all the time he had been spending indoors which was to blame for his pallor. She listened as he began to speak.

"Most people know that the Battle of Roliça marked the victory of Sir Arthur Wellesley's army over that of the General of Division, Henri François, Comte Delaborde, and the Imperial French. It was England's first battle in the war."

James turned to her. She met his gaze.

"I confess I did not. But pray, go on."

"I was under the command of Colonel Lake." James' brow furrowed deeply and Charlotte could see the strain it was placing on him to recount the story. She wondered whether she should tell him to stop, and not torture himself on her account. But she wanted to know the truth, so she said nothing, and James continued. "We tried to outflank the French twice during the day, and each time they had the sense to fall back. Colonel Lake became frustrated and decided to act. In his haste, he led us up a gully toward where the French were positioned. Unfortunately, we arrived after Delaborde had achieved a position of advantage. It was a massacre - Colonel Lake was killed, as were most of my regiment. I barely survived. Ironically enough, what saved me was my injuries, for the French believed me too bloody to be alive, and left me. I was lucky that one of Wellesley's troop was diligent enough to check the bodies on the field, and found that I was still breathing."

Charlotte hesitated to ask her next question.

"And your face?"

"The result of a Frenchman's sword. When our rifles were empty, we took to the blade. He was very skilled with it - much more so than I, I'm afraid. It was only by the grace of God that my life was saved. And it was a blessing that my sword bested his."

"You killed him?"

James stopped and Charlotte faced him.

"It was war, Charlotte. People died. If I had not done so, he would have killed me."

She was silent. Charlotte knew that it had been war, but the thought of James killing someone seemed impossible. He was the kindest man she knew. His gentle nature and caring manner had always endeared him to her, and she could never imagine him taking anyone's life, even though she knew that he must have. It still did not align with her perception of him in her mind.

She whispered.

"Why did you not tell me you were alive?"

"I could not," James answered.

"Why not?" she protested.

"For the first few months of my recuperation, I simply couldn't do it. And after that, my dear Charlotte, I was more a monster then than I am now. My face was horrible, frightful. I did not want anyone to see me, as those who did were repelled. You have no idea what it was like to endure. The moment someone saw my face they turned away because their stomachs could not handle the sight of me. Children cried and ran away."

"James..."

"I did not want you to see me," he reiterated. "It took months for me to recover, and by the time I had

purchased passage home, I had also heard of your engagement to the Earl of Benton. It seemed fitting. You would
be a lady of great importance, as you should be. I could
not interfere."

"It would have been no interference," Charlotte
protested.

James smiled slightly.

"I almost came here. When the wedding was
approaching. I had the terrible urge to come here and see
you. I made my way to the woods on the outskirts of the
property, near the gardens, and hid there, but I could not
make myself go any further. I thought better of my
actions, and I believed you would be happier with Lord
Benton. And, in truth, I think I was right. What I did that
day was for the best - Malcolm Tate gave you what I
could not."

Charlotte frowned.

"Why not?"

James shook his head.

"You have had a happy life. You have a son. You have
the freedom to go where you please with no intrusive
looks or horrified expressions. I could not give you that.
As the Countess of Benton, you could go anywhere you
chose without restraint or discomfort. My life is restricted
to the property lines of Watton Hall. I go no further. The
places I see the most are those which I have seen for most
of my life – the walls of my home. They are all that I
have."

The sadness in his voice and the view of the world
which he now held was heart-breaking. This was not the
James she knew – that James was a man who was never

restrained, who did things wholeheartedly, and without hesitation. He had traveled to defend king and country, never fearing for his own harm.

It was not at all reasonable that he should suffer such censure because of what those efforts had inflicted upon him.

Charlotte took his hand and gripped his fingers gently.

"No longer, James. You have more than the walls of your home. You have William. You have Caldor House. And you have me."

CHAPTER ELEVEN

Three weeks later

James became, once again, a frequent visitor to Caldor House, and on this particular day, the sun was shining brightly on him as he and Charlotte played shuttlecock. His coat was off and the racquet felt good in his hand. William kept score, with little George seated on his lap watching.

"Another point down, Charlotte," William called as the shuttle fell to the floor once more.

"No fair," Charlotte protested. "I was distracted by George's giggling."

"Not a good enough excuse," William countered.

"You've always favored James over me," Charlotte continued with a laugh. "Ever since we were children."

"I protest," James interrupted. He smiled broadly at her. "As I recall, it was the other way around. Your brother always favored you when we were children. After all, he is your brother. My fortunes now are purely due to my efforts."

Charlotte chuckled.

"I have my version, and it is the one I am holding to. You are trying to cheat, James Watts!" she laughed.

"Never!" James protested merrily.

He almost didn't recognise his own voice. It had been so long since he'd had a reason for joy. In the past few weeks, his reasons had multiplied and he knew exactly who was responsible for that.

"Mama!" George called for Charlotte. He raised his small hands in the air, closing and opening his palms to her.

Charlotte set her racquet aside.

"I believe that we must take a break from this match. It seems that we have an unexpected interruption."

She crossed the lawn and went to her brother, plucking George from his hands. The child nestled against her immediately as James stood silently and watched.

Charlotte and George were a walking dream to him. Watching the woman he cared for, with her son, knowing it was a picture devoid of a husband and father, was almost mesmerizing. James found that he couldn't help but watch them with great fondness. He'd always known Charlotte would be a good mother, but she was better than anything he could have imagined.

George's love for his mother was apparent, as was the case was with every child, at least at first. However, Charlotte's devotion to her son was remarkable, especially for someone who'd had little maternal care in her own life. His stepmother had done her best, but she was not Charlotte's mother.

The child began to fret and Charlotte cooed to soothe him.

"I think it is time for his lunch," she informed them. "And so, we shall be going inside."

"Very well," said James with good humor.

William got to his feet and strode toward the house, following his sister. James collected his jacket and caught up with them on the lawn and they all entered the house together.

The staff at Caldor House were beginning to get used to his presence, James thought, although the stares continued.

"James, would you hold George please?"

James stopped short at the question. He looked at Charlotte in surprise.

"Me?"

She grinned.

"Yes, you. I need to see about his food. Cook does not like it when I bring him into the kitchen."

She passed her son to James, who didn't know what to do. He took the child, holding him gingerly.

William looked at him and made no effort to hide the grin on his face.

"This suits you," he said.

James gave William an accusing look. He then realized that George was staring at him.

George's big eyes were drinking him in. A moment later his tiny hands followed the path that his eyes had taken, as he reached up to hold James' face and inspected it carefully. James was breathless. No one ever touched his face. Absolutely no one. He didn't allow it. However, how could he tell a three-year-old not to touch? Instead, he stood stunned, as the child looked at him without fear or tears. Then George did something completely unexpected. He put his small arms around James' neck and hugged him, nestling into the crook of his shoulder. He was still there when his mother returned.

Charlotte walked back into the room and stopped at the sight of her son with James. A broad smile spread across her face. She went towards them.

"It seems that George is very fond of you."

"It would seem so," James replied. He passed the child to his mother.

Charlotte settled George on her hip.

"And you, James? Are you fond of George?"

A lump formed in his throat.

"Of course I am."

Charlotte's smile grew.

"I am awfully glad to hear it. It is time for George's tea. I shall find you both in a little while."

She looked at him with brilliant eyes and then turned to leave the room.

William walked up beside him.

"I told you I was right."

"Right?"

"That it was time you allowed Charlotte back into your life. The past few weeks have been much happier for you than all of the ones before, since the day you came back from the war. Do not deny it. It is written all over your face."

"William."

"I told you. Do not deny it. You cannot hide it. Perhaps now, with George's approval and the renewal of our friendships, you might feel at liberty to make the feelings of your heart known to my sister."

James balked at the suggestion. However, he had no chance to respond, as William quickly excused himself to go upstairs.

"I will meet you in the music room. I promised Miss Durand that I would entertain her today, and I must assist her down the stairs."

"Very well," James replied.

He watched his friend as he departed. Mary Durand, the young woman whom the family had taken in, was now making a marvelous, almost miraculous recovery and had finally revealed her last name to them. The hardest part, once the illness had passed, was to restore her strength, which was unfortunately severely lacking. The physician had said that years of neglect and lack of food was the cause, and he also alluded to the fact that she appeared to have suffered some mistreatment. Miss Durand neither denied nor confirmed it, but the truth was apparent to all who saw her.

James patiently strolled towards the music room. It would take William some time to assist Miss Durand, for the stairs were quite tall, and the upstairs hallway long. Charlotte would need time to feed her child. So, there was no rush. Instead, he walked quietly through the house, perusing the paintings that lined the walls and thinking of what William had suggested.

The day he had come to check on Charlotte's health had changed everything for him. He'd had no intention of staying, but he had. He had not intended to tell her what had happened to him, yet he had. He blamed that upon the relief of knowing that she was well and not in harm's way, even though what had followed was entirely his own choice.

James had found a great relief in admitting the truth to Charlotte and seeing the acceptance in her eyes. She had not pressed him when they'd talked – she'd asked questions and, if he had refused to answer, she'd accepted that. However, the more they had talked that day, the more he had wanted to tell her. He'd felt freed from a great weight, simply from the act of telling her.

He hated to admit it because it made it very clear what a waste all of the years he'd spent hidden away had been, but his father was correct. Charlotte was nothing like others he'd encountered. She saw him. Not his scars or his pain. Him.

Those thoughts were a comfort to him, and they made him stronger, better able to bear the stares and the whispers. He also had to admit that, since his resumption of visits to Caldor House, the staff had slowly become more accustomed to his presence, and no longer stared or whispered quite as much.

James was entertaining the thought that life could, perhaps, be normal again. Then, he caught a glimpse of himself in the large ornate mirror which hung in the hallway on the way to the music room.

His face looked like the irregular sewing of a novice who had no conception of straight lines nor any technique. The field surgeon had done his best to repair his face, but there was no remedy for the scars.

No matter what she makes you think or feel, this who you are.

James turned away.

They gathered in the music room an hour later. George was with his nurse, Mrs. White, in the nursery although James had hoped he would join them. The child's exuberance and merriment was a welcome addition to their gatherings. If he could, he would be a witness to the child's growing up. He was sure that George would make quite a man someday.

James sat alone in the chair which faced the door, while William occupied the piano bench. His friend was happily playing his favorite pieces, while his sister and Miss Durand listened. Mary Durand was a curious specimen, James thought.

Her dark blonde hair was limp, lifeless, though it held the hint of a natural curl, which was no doubt the result of her lack of nourishment. In the weeks since her arrival at Caldor House, though, her face had filled out to make a more appealing image. Her cheeks were freckled, something which some might see as detracting from her appearance, though James did not regard them so and suspected that, once she had recovered further, she would be quite a beautiful woman.

One thing he had noted, however, was that her dark blue eyes seemed always fixed on one spot. William.

James smiled to himself. It seemed that Miss Durand

LOVING THE SCARRED SOLDIER | 139

had developed some degree of admiration for her savior. He hid his grin, but Charlotte noticed it nonetheless and gave him a questioning look. James shook his head, hoping to avoid explaining himself.

It did not work.

Charlotte left Mary on the chaise and came to sit on the chair beside him.

"What amuses you?"

He turned to her and smiled.

"Nothing you need concern yourself with."

"Oh no, James Watts. You cannot get rid of me so easily. Something just elicited a smile from you. What was it?"

The glimmer of mischievous delight in Charlotte's eyes was enticing. His hand twitched with the desire to touch her cheek the way he once had. He balled his hand into a fist instead and diverted both of them by teasing her.

"I cannot tell you."

"You will not tell me," Charlotte corrected him. "And why not? What secrets do you have from me, James?"

Far too many.

"None."

She shook her head.

"In that case, you must tell me. What secrets should there be between friends? Do you not agree, Mary?"

The young woman startled at her name. Her tone was coarse but she was pleasant nonetheless.

"With what, Lady Benton?"

Charlotte smiled.

"What have I told you, Mary? Please, call me Charlotte."

Mary's cheeks rose in a brilliant smile.

"Charlotte. What was your question?"

Charlotte repeated herself.

"Should there be secrets amongst friends?"

"Only if the truth would do more harm than good," Mary replied.

Her response struck him as insightful. Did Mary Durand feel as he did - that the person she cared for and admired was beyond her? She glanced in William's direction. His friend seemed completely oblivious to their discourse. Seeing that, James knew that his suspicions were accurate.

"I do not think so," Charlotte countered. "I think that honesty is always the best policy. Secrets only bring pain, whether now or later, and in most cases, the longer it takes for the truth to be revealed, the more painful it is."

Charlotte looked at him. James could not respond, for it was obvious what she was implying.

"Do you truly think so, Charlotte?" Mary questioned.

She was only nineteen, and from what James could tell, she was not accustomed to company.

"I do," Charlotte confirmed. "I believe that truth only heals, even if it must sometimes hurt to do so."

"Would you all stop this debating and listen to me play?" William interjected. His hands never left the keys. "I am playing a very difficult movement of James Hook and I am playing it quite skillfully, in my opinion. And you are drowning out the sound with your merry conversation."

There was a laugh in his voice and James chuckled.

"Sorry, my good man. We beg your forgiveness. We will pay the utmost attention from now on."

Mary immediately refocused her attention on William, but Charlotte did not. She kept her eyes on James and reached out to take his hand.

"James," she whispered. "Let us not have secrets from one another."

His lips remained sealed. He could not express agreement with what she had asked – to do so would be a lie and he did not wish to lie.

"Please?"

He took her hand in his and looked at her delicate fingers.

"Do not ask me to make a promise which I cannot keep, Charlotte. I do not want to lie to you."

"Then we are of the same mind. Why then can you not promise to keep no secrets?"

He raised his eyes to hers but instead was met by her father's gaze. The Duke was surreptitiously looking through the gap of the slightly open door. James gave no indication that he had noticed, and did not reveal to the others that they were being watched. He turned his eyes back to Charlotte's face, which was filled with an odd combination of sadness and hope.

"Because, I have to keep some secrets, Charlotte. There are simply things I cannot say."

Charlotte withdrew her hand and moved away from him. She settled on the chaise beside Mary, a sad expression in her eyes, and the bright hopefulness he had seen earlier was completely gone from her countenance.

I am sorry, Charlotte. I cannot tell you everything. I cannot tell you how I feel, for it would be of no use to either of us. I cannot be the man you need. I am not the man who others would want for you.

James glanced back towards the door and found that it was now firmly closed.

CHAPTER TWELVE

William finished playing the sonata and took the seat Charlotte had left vacant beside James. She could not look at her former love. It was too difficult. Seeing her son with him, and seeing him smile again, was everything she wanted. Every time she thought there was hope, he retreated again.

James had to feel what she did. He could not be as impervious as he pretended to be. She saw him. She saw his eyes. He felt the same way but refused to admit it.

Why does he deny us both?

Charlotte thought that the weeks since his first visit to Caldor House had changed something. It certainly had in her. Once again, she knew what it felt like to be alive - James had brought her back to life. What's more, George adored him. Her son needed a man in his life, a man who was not his grandfather or uncle, but a man who could be a father to him. Charlotte could not deny that seeing them together that day had made her think of the possibilities.

His supposed death had separated them, but his resurrection had revived the love that was.

Always was.

She looked at James.

And always will be.

James was always the man she had seen herself marrying, who she had seen as the father to her children, in every dream of her future. Though George would not be of his blood, she did not doubt that James would love the child as his own. He would help George become the man he was meant to be and to be ready to take on the responsibilities of his title. If only James would allow himself to be that kind of man, to fulfill his own potential.

Why is he blind to what I see? Why does he believe himself less than who he was before when I think of him now as so much more than I did before? He only sees his face. I see the man whose heart still beats for those he cares for, and whose honor has never faltered.

As if drawn by her thoughts, James looked in her direction. Charlotte's skin tingled as if a cold wind blew across it. Neither could look away. There was so much in his eyes – so much that he did not, would not put into words. Charlotte could see his care for her. She could see the tangled pattern of affection and fear. He feared feeling what he did. That was why he would not make the promise she had asked for. He knew she would make him confess his secrets and the truth of his feelings. She would not stop until he did so, and they both knew what was in the other's heart.

I cannot tell you unless you first reveal yourself to me.

This time I will best you, James. This time I will win and you will yield.

James held her gaze. A smile slowly crept across his face. Charlotte did her best to smile as well. Thankfully, William drew James' attention away from her, before Charlotte's emotions overwhelmed her.

"You must see it," her brother commented.

"See what?" Charlotte interjected.

Her brother glanced in her direction.

"The new rifle I purchased last week while I was in town. It's a marvelous piece. Quite exceptional."

Charlotte chuckled.

"You are talking of firearms?"

"Yes," William replied. "What are you discussing?"

Charlotte looked at Mary. They smiled at one another and answered simultaneously.

"Nothing."

Her brother shook his head.

"I think that I know the cause of that answer." He got to his feet. "It is because we men are here disturbing you. I think it time that we leave these ladies to their conversation. What do you think, James?"

James rose and stood beside him, smiling.

"I think you have the right idea, William. Charlotte and Miss Durand do not need us to prevent the conversations which they would be having if we were not here. I think it a good idea for you to show me that rifle of yours."

"I think that I agree." William bowed exaggeratedly to Charlotte and Miss Durand. "We will leave you now. I shall return later to assist Miss Durand back to her room." His attention turned to Mary. "I hope to see you out of your room more, Miss Durand, now that you are recovering your strength."

Mary's cheeks turned red and her eyes shifted focus to her lap.

"I hope to be, my Lord."

William laughed. "Please call me William," he said.

Charlotte was proud of her brother. His kindness to Mary was unprecedented, given their father's dislike of her presence. Despite his numerous attempts to get William to turn her from the house, William refused to entertain the idea, and their father, remarkably, did not invoke his absolute authority.

William treated the fragile young woman as an equal in social standing. Charlotte prayed that her father would continue to tolerate Miss Durand's presence, however unwillingly.

The men bowed their heads and exited the room, leaving Charlotte and Mary alone. The young woman's cheeks were still red.

"My brother is quite fond of you," Charlotte commented.

Mary's eyes flew up to meets hers, and her tone was almost panicked.

"No, he is not. I assure you! If he has conceived of such a thing, I certainly have given him no encouragement."

Charlotte's brow wrinkled at her adamant response, then she smiled gently.

"Mary, what do you think I mean? William sees you much as he sees me. He cares for you as he would care for me if it were I who was in your position. There is nothing wrong with that."

"Yes," Mary replied. "Like a sister is what you meant?"

"Yes, as a sister. What did you think I meant?"

"Nothing."

Charlotte studied Mary's expression. There was a look on her face of almost disappointment. Her cheek was flushed, and Charlotte momentarily worried that her fever had returned. But then she realized Mary was blushing.

Why would she think...Oh my!

Charlotte looked at Mary sympathetically. Of course. How had she missed it? Mary admired William.

She placed a gentle hand on Mary's shoulder.

"And if it was as something more than a sister, there would be nothing wrong in that either, I dare say."

Mary looked at her stunned. "Do you mean it?"

"I do. Mary, we are all people. It does not matter what class or creed we are. We are all the same. We all need closeness, love, and affection. No one is immune to such feelings. Even if others would wish us not to have them."

"Like your father?"

Charlotte's lips parted as she momentarily considered her response.

"My father is a man with very specific ideas. I do not adhere to them and my brother does not either, at least not entirely."

"Entirely?"

Charlotte could see the hope that glimmered reluctantly in Mary's eyes. She hated to disappoint her, but she had to caution her.

"My brother has his own mind, but I fear that my father influences him more than he does me. There are some things that are more difficult for William to refuse, where I am able to do so. He is our father's heir. He has many demands upon him."

Charlotte watched defeat spread across Mary's face. Her voice was subdued when she spoke again.

"I understand."

She hated to see what her words had done to Mary, but she had to be truthful. It was what she'd said earlier. The truth, even if it caused pain, would only make things easier in the end. Mary might be slightly infatuated with William, but there was no way her father would allow a union.

He will not accept James. Father deemed him beneath me before he was injured and would be even less likely to condone a match now. He would be even less willing to accept Mary. We do not even know her parentage. It is an unfair thing, but it is the world we live in. Charlotte sighed. *I hope I can help her find a good situation.*

"Charlotte?"

Charlotte was lost in her thoughts, completely oblivious to the fact that Mary was staring at her.

"Yes?" Charlotte replied quickly. "Forgive me, I was wool-gathering."

Mary smiled. "I asked if you enjoyed the time outside."

Charlotte smiled. "Indeed, I did," she patted Mary's

hand gently. "You will soon be able to join us. A few more weeks and you will be yourself again."

Mary lowered her eyes. "I do not want to be who I was before. I want to be different."

Charlotte's curiosity got the better of her.

"What was your life like before? You have not told any of us. Forgive me if I am prying, I only want to help."

"I know that you do. I know you all do," Mary replied sadly. "I just... it is very difficult. There was so much pain and hurt."

Charlotte squeezed her hand comfortingly.

"You can tell me as much or as little as you want. Do not feel pressured."

Mary met her gaze. Charlotte could see the unshed tears in her eyes.

"You have no idea what it was like. I had no clothes and hardly any food. I slept in a corner of the scullery so that I would not be seen by others. I worked, cleaning the house day and night. They worked me so hard and fed me so little."

Anger began to burn in Charlotte's veins.

"Who did this to you, Mary? Who would treat you in such an abominable way?"

"My aunt and uncle."

Charlotte felt as if she'd been slapped. She stammered her response, incredulous.

"Your aunt and uncle?"

Mary nodded silently, then swallowed and began to speak again.

"My father, Peter Durand, left me in Tynson when he went off to make a better life, to earn enough that we might have better things. He asked my uncle and aunt to care for me. That was nine years ago. He has never returned, though he used to write often."

"Do you know what happened to him?" Charlotte questioned.

"No, I do not know. He said he was going to America two years ago. I have heard nothing of him since. That was why I ran away. I could no longer bear their treatment of me. I was determined to find my father. I thought I could manage it, but I was so tired and weak, and unable to pay for the coach, and so I had to walk."

"Where were you going?"

"To London, to the docks at Tilbury. I hoped to take a ship there."

Charlotte balked.

"You were trying to get to London from Tynson? Do you have an idea how far that is?"

Mary shook her head.

"No. Is it very far?"

She could not believe her ears.

"Mary, that is a couple of days travel in a carriage and more than a week's walk, in good weather, even without the storms we have had. You could not possibly travel that far on foot, and alone." Mary's expression was sheepish. It was clear that the poor girl had set out with no idea of how far she was going. She had just been desperate to escape. "Perhaps William can help?"

"How?"

"My brother knows many people in London. He might be able to get information on your father's location.

There is little point in going to London if he is still in America."

Mary shook her head.

"I have been a fool. I thought that I could search for news of him when I got there."

"Mary, London is a very large place and dangerous for a young woman alone."

Tears began to fill Mary's eyes as her head bowed lower.

"You must think me terribly foolish not to know these things. I would not blame you if you did."

"No. Of course not," Charlotte assured her. "I would never think that."

"Why not? I am foolish. I have had little education or understanding. I thought I could walk to London when I do not even know the distance." The tears rolled down her cheeks. "What was I thinking, to even try?"

Charlotte moved closer to hug her and patted Mary's back comfortingly.

"Do not cry, Mary. I do not think any less of you. I do not think you foolish. You are just unaccustomed to the world."

Mary would not hear it.

"I am foolish. I have learned nothing since I was a small child and even then I had the simplest of educations. My father was always working and taught me what he could when he had the time, but he was more preoccupied with putting food on the table and keeping a roof over our heads."

Immense pity filled Charlotte's heart. Mary had suffered so much, it hardly seemed fair - she was still a girl, yet she had endured more than most did in a lifetime.

"I promise you we will help you, Mary. Truly, I swear it."

Charlotte stated her promise just as her brother returned to the room. He stared at them, a look of concern crossing his face.

"What has happened?"

Mary immediately pulled away from her and attempted to wipe the tears from her cheeks. Charlotte stood and went to her brother, sure that Mary would appreciate the time to compose herself before he saw her.

She pulled William aside, whilst James remained in the doorway, as if unsure whether he should intrude.

"What has happened?" William repeated his question quietly.

Charlotte could barely meet his eye. She looked at Mary instead.

"Mary told me what happened to her, before you found her."

William was incredulous. "What did she say?"

Charlotte nodded. "She told me everything. Who hurt her and why she was on the road when you found her? It was a horrible tale."

"What was said?"

She shook her head. "Not now. I think it best for her to return to bed and rest."

"Charlotte?" William insisted. "Tell me now!" His voice betrayed his emotions, and Charlotte, taken aback with his adamance, sat back down and sighed.

She took a deep breath and recounted Mary's tale.

Her brother's face was ghostly pale after hearing it. He looked at Mary, who continued to keep her face turned away from them.

"Insufferable people. Who could treat another in such a manner? And a family member, no less."

"Please, William. Do not say anything to her. She is very upset at the moment. I told her we would help her."

"I will do whatever I can to find her father," her brother assured her.

Charlotte smiled.

"I knew you would, William. Now, let's get her back to her bed-chamber so that she can rest. We can speak more of this later."

William walked to the chaise to collect Mary, while Charlotte stood at the door with James. Neither said anything. What needed to be said would not be uttered, not then, at least.

CHAPTER THIRTEEN

J ames was eagerly waiting on the front steps of
Watton Hall when William and Charlotte stepped
down from their carriage. They had informed him
of their intention to meet with him, and his father, to
discuss the matter of Mary Durand. Given their own
father's opinions on the subject, they had thought it best
to confer at Watton Hall. James greeted them, smiling.

"Good morning!"

"Good morning!" William and Charlotte chorused.

His friend was dressed in grey, while Charlotte was
in a lovely peach-toned dress with white trim around the
neckline and sleeves. Her dark hair was adorned by a
ribbon that matched her dress, and a bright smile illuminated her face. It warmed his heart to see it.

They bowed to each other politely. James offered his
arm, and Charlotte took it.

"You look lovely, my dear."

Her cheeks reddened.

"Thank you, James," she said.

They walked into the house, where the sound of men hard at work filled the air.

"What's all this?" William asked as he gave his coat to the footman.

"Improvements," James answered. "Father thinks it is time to do the repairs he has put off for the past few years." He sighed. "I am to blame for that. He did not want workmen in the house previously, on my behalf."

Charlotte squeezed his arm.

"Well, that is all at an end now."

James nodded.

"Yes. It is."

They walked to his father's office, where Mr. Watts waited, expecting them. His father bowed politely and then stepped forward to shake William's hand.

"Good morning, Lord William. Lady Charlotte. How are you today?"

"Very well, John. Yourself?" William replied.

"I am quite well. Beatrice is herself again." He smiled at Charlotte. "Thanks to the efforts of this young lady. Business is thriving, my son is up and about and my favorite young people are here to visit me. What more could I ask for?"

"That sounds wonderful," Charlotte commented.

His father took her hand from his arm and led her to a chair. James and William sat nearby, while his father went back to sit behind his desk.

"Now, tell me. What brings you here today?"

William was the first to speak.

"Well, some weeks ago, I found a destitute young woman along the road from here to Caldor House. My family took her in and cared for her - her name is Mary Durand. She is but nineteen years old but she has suffered terribly at the hands of a neglectful aunt and uncle, who were supposed to care for her. She ran away from that situation in the hopes of finding her father, who, as she was last informed, in America."

His father shook his head.

"I see. A sad case. What can I do to help?"

"We would ask you to use your connections in London to help us locate Miss Durand's father," James replied. "William and Charlotte would like to see her to safe accommodation once she is fit enough to leave their home, which we pray will be soon."

"Yes," Charlotte agreed. "We do not want her to leave and find herself in the same pitiful state she came to us. She had no clothes but those on her back and little money to survive on, yet her desperation drove her on an almost impossible journey on foot."

His father's eyes snapped up from his pensive state.

"Did you say she traveled on foot?"

Charlotte nodded.

"Yes, Mr. Watts. On foot."

"And from where was she traveling?"

"Tynson."

"Tynson? Such a long distance. And on foot!" His father was incredulous.

"John, that, in itself tells you from what kind of circumstance the girl was escaping," William interjected. Concern was in his eyes and there was thoughtfulness in his expression. "Charlotte tells me she had no idea of the distance she was traveling, only that she had to escape. We are seeking your help to help her."

His father was silent for several seconds, and James could see him contemplating as he sat, motionless. Finally, he spoke.

"What is her father's name and what is his profession?"

"Peter Durand. He is in manufacturing and has some interest in invention, and traveled to America perhaps two years ago," William explained. "I do not know much else."

"It is a start. I will contact my associates in London. Mr. Theodore Pyke has interests in manufacturing and has many connections in Boston and New York. I am sure that he would be able to help." He met William's gaze. "It may take some time to find her father if we can find him at all. Might you be prepared to have the young lady under your roof that long?"

William smiled slightly.

"You mean to ask if our father will allow it?"

His father nodded.

"Yes. The Duke is not the kind of man who allows guests for very long."

His father was trying to be mild, but James knew what he meant, and he was sure that Charlotte and William did as well. Mary was not of their class. The Duke would never allow her to stay once she was well. He had barely been convinced to permit her presence during her convalescence.

"Never fear, I will take care of that." William's words were firm. "She will stay with us for as long as it takes."

"Are you sure, William?" Charlotte questioned. "Father might prove difficult about her."

William looked at his sister, resolve in his eyes.

"I shall take care of it. Miss Durand will not leave our house until she has somewhere safe to go to."

She smiled brightly.

"I am glad you are taking this position. I too am adamant that Mary will not leave us until she has somewhere suitable to go. Regardless of what Father says, I will not allow her to leave us."

William smiled.

"Neither will I."

James' father smiled broadly.

"Very well. If you are prepared to keep her safe. I am prepared to help you." His father turned to him. "James, you had several acquaintances in industry. Why do you not contact them?"

James was momentarily at a loss for words. His father was asking him to contact others and to reveal his existence to them. He knew what that would mean: they would want to see him. They would eventually come to Watton Hall and he would have to face the looks on their faces when they saw him. He swallowed and looked at Charlotte taking in the hopeful look in her eyes. He knew he had to help, regardless of the cost to him.

"Yes, Father. I shall write to them today."

He met Charlotte's eyes, and there was nothing but delight in them. She knew that he was doing this for her - he cared about Miss Durand, for she was a sweet girl, a bit naïve, but good-natured, but it wasn't her interests that propelled him to action. It was Charlotte's.

He smiled at Charlotte politely.

I would do anything for you.

Charlotte was a different woman now and James could see it. As a girl, she had been a bit rebellious, but now she was more than that – she was outspoken. She was still determined, but now she had a purpose outside of herself. The way she was coming to Miss Durand's aid was proof of that.

Her compassion had grown over the years.

It only makes me admire her more, he thought to himself.

His father rose.

"Now, if we are all in agreement, then I think we can adjourn this meeting," His father said. Everyone nodded. "Very well. James, would you take Lady Charlotte out into the gardens? I have some private matters to discuss with William."

His father did not need to repeat the request, for James was more than happy to spend time alone with Charlotte. They both rose, and, offering his arm, he left with Charlotte, smiling broadly.

This time there was no companion to play chaperone and watch over them, though as Charlotte was a widow, it was not so necessary anymore. It felt like they were children again when they had roamed the halls and gardens of Watton Hall unchaperoned. They'd run through the grounds in the sun, and done such things as sliding along the corridors on the rugs, often falling over themselves. They had been, he thought now, rather unruly. His father, though respectable, was not as strict as the Duke of Mormont. He had understood that children needed to be children occasionally, and not the miniature replicas of the men and women they were destined to become. It was not a common point of view with some, but it suited them entirely.

Once in view of the household, Charlotte clasped her hands in front of her. James wished for her hand on his arm and missed the feeling of their connection, but he could not insist upon it. It would be wrong to do so.

"I must say, William surprised me," Charlotte muttered absently. "I did not think he would take such a stand on Mary's behalf, especially since our father is quite adamant to the contrary."

James smiled. Perhaps the admiration Mary had was not one-sided, he thought. Then again, it may simply have been William's chivalrous nature being aroused. He'd never had such a situation present itself before now. Raised at Caldor House, and in the best of society, William knew little of hardship and suffering. It was a distant thing to him, a thing which his father addressed as a charitable endeavor undertaken once a month, with a donation to the parish support fund. James believed that through Mary, suffering had become something real to William, perhaps for the first time, rather than being the plight of the unknown, it was now that of someone he had to watch over and care for.

"I think your brother has developed splendidly in his thinking."

"I believe you might be right. When we were

younger, he would never have dreamt of standing up to father."

James nodded.

"He is no longer a boy, Charlotte. William is a man and it is time he found his footing. Though I expect he still has some way to go. Your father's influence is a powerful one and not easily broken."

The sound of Charlotte's sigh was a light in the air.

"You know James, I pity William sometimes. Father has placed the weight of the world upon him. I worry he might not be able to bear it."

James took her hand tenderly and squeezed it.

"That is why he has us to lean on. We must always be there for him."

A smile crept across her face.

"Then we will always be there for him."

They continued walking in the garden until a sprinkle of light rain caused them to retreat indoors. They went to the library, and Charlotte settled herself on the chaise. James retrieved a book from the shelf and sat on the other end of the chaise.

"May I read this to you?"

"What is it?" Charlotte questioned. She peered at the book in his hands.

James smiled.

"Poetry."

Charlotte giggled.

"You read poetry? When we were children, I had to force you to so much as pick up a book of poetry."

"Yes, well I have grown up, Charlotte. As have you. I

learned the value of words, especially since I have had little else to do for the past few years."

His words were light-hearted. But his time alone had changed him more than he had initially realized. Poetry had been abhorrent to him in his youth, but as he grew older, he had found comfort in the well-weighed word.

"This book was published a few years ago. Shelley and his friend Thomas Hogg wrote it during their time at Oxford, so the legend goes. It's called 'The Posthumous Fragments of Margaret Nicholson.'"

Charlotte looked stunned. "Was she not the woman who made an attempt on the life of King George?"

James smiled. "The very one." He flipped the book open. "Listen." He began to read and Charlotte sat silently listening.

"STAY ye days of contentment and joy,

Whilst love every care is erasing,

Stay ye pleasures that never can cloy,

And ye spirits that can never cease pleasing.

And if any soft passion be near,

Which mortals, frail mortals, can know,

Let love shed on the bosom a tear,

And dissolve the chill ice-drop of woe."

"It's beautiful," said Charlotte, a tear glistening on her cheek.

"And frightfully accurate," said James, wiping the tear from her cheek. He went on reading, page after page as she continued listening to him. He was consumed by the words and it took him a moment to realize that she was staring at him.

He smiled.

"What are you staring at?"

Charlotte's cheeks turned crimson. She turned away. "Nothing."

"Not nothing," James insisted. "What is it?"

Charlotte still refused to answer. He set the book down beside him and took her hand. Her reaction was immediate. She turned and met his gaze, her chocolate eyes so piercing that James couldn't tear his eyes away. His gaze drifted from her eyes to her lips, which parted slightly, and James felt a lump form in his throat at the sight.

He had to tear himself away before temptation led him to do something he shouldn't.

"There is another poem I would like to read to you."

"I would love to hear it."

James could feel her eyes watching him as he walked to the shelf to retrieve another book. He came back and sat beside her again.

"This one is a favorite of mine," he informed her.

Charlotte smiled.

"I cannot wait to hear it, if that is so."

"'By thy pale beams I solitary rove,

To thee my tender grief confide;

Serenely sweet you gild the silent grove,

My friend, my goddess, and my guide.'"

The words of Lady Mary Wortley Montagu slipped from his lips. Countless times, James had imagined speaking these words to Charlotte, and now, seeing Charlotte's expression as he told her that they epitomized what he felt for her, he was overcome. He met her gaze and lost himself in her eyes.

I love you Charlotte. You are my friend, my goddess, and my guide. You have brought me out of the darkness. I could not have done it without you. I need you by my side, Charlotte. I cannot be with you, but I cannot be apart from you.

CHAPTER FOURTEEN

A week later

C harlotte's heart was racing as she slipped her pearl
comb through her hair. Delight filled her heart and
her hands trembled as she finished her preparations.
There was a knock on the door and Sophie answered it.
The nursemaid entered.

Charlotte stopped her preparation to greet the
woman.

"Mrs. White, is George asleep already?"

"Yes, Lady Benton. Is there anything else you will
need tonight? If not, I would like to retire. I am not
feeling my best."

"Of course," Charlotte replied, concerned. "I will
look in on George later. Get your rest. If he wakes, I shall
take care of him."

The nurse nodded her head. "Thank you, my Lady."

Mrs. White left the room, and Charlotte sat on the edge of her bed. She had to calm herself. She could not remember the last time her heart had beaten so quickly - she had to catch her breath.

"Are you alright, Charlotte?" Sophie stood by her side. "Are you feeling unwell?"

She shook her head. "To the contrary. I have never felt better."

"But madame, you are flushed." Sophie placed her hand on Charlotte's forehead. "But you do not have a fever."

"It is not illness that reddens my cheeks," Charlotte confessed.

Sophie smiled knowingly.

"Then I must presume it has something to do with our special dinner guest?"

Charlotte looked up at her friend.

"Sophie, I cannot tell you how it felt to have him accept my invitation. He has avoided our father at all costs, but tonight he is willing to dine with us. And then there was that beautiful poem he read to me. Sophie, I swear he was speaking only to me, that he was trying to tell me how he felt. I could see it in his eyes, even though he never said it directly."

Sophie sighed.

"You two seem to operate in riddles. Would not honesty and forthrightness be a better approach? You care for one another tenderly. Why hide it?"

Charlotte couldn't answer. Perhaps it was because she still feared another rejection. If James was not yet ready to accept her affection and refused her again, denying what they both felt, what use was there in saying anything?

"Charlotte, you do intend to tell him how you feel, don't you? It's the very least you could do."

She couldn't look at her companion. "It is not that simple, Sophie."

"Ah! You English women! Why must all things be so complicated?"

"Because it is not just a matter of a mere declaration. There is also my father to contend with on the matter. Though I should feel nothing, when faced with my father's disapprobation, I cannot say that James would feel nothing. He is still getting used to the real world again. This dinner is only the first step, and his aid to Mary, another. I do not want to rush him. I also do not want to get ahead of myself. If anyone must declare their feelings it must be him."

Sophie frowned. "And what if he does not?"

"Then we shall remain in this purgatory together, ever by each other's side yet not as one."

Sophie's hand closed around hers. "Then I shall pray that he has the words you wish to hear. I daresay it would be torture for you both otherwise."

Charlotte smiled. "Thank you, Sophie. You are marvelous."

She resumed her preparation before going to check on Mary. Mary would not be joining them for dinner, as her father did not permit it, given that a guest was expected. He did not want to have to explain her presence; even though Charlotte had made it clear to him that she had already explained the situation to James many times.

She strolled down the hall to Mary's room, where she found the young woman seated in the window seat with a book in her hand.

Charlotte smiled. "Are you reading?"

Mary closed the book quickly, shoving it between her body and the cushions that surrounded her. Her cheeks became pink.

"I was just looking. I did not take it."

Charlotte sat beside her in the seat. "I did not imagine you did. I merely asked if you were reading, my dear."

Mary's eyes fell. "I was only looking at it. I wondered what the story might be. You have ever so many books here."

Charlotte picked up the book and placed it in Mary's hands.

"You should read it then."

Mary set the book on her lap, her cheeks flushed.

"I cannot read very well, Charlotte. Books were a luxury in my aunt and uncle's house, and one we could not afford. This book is more advanced than I can manage. My father taught me to read and write a little before he left, but only the basics. But he wanted me to grow up to be a regular lady."

Although her father had surely meant the best for her, he could have had no idea what he would be subjecting his daughter to by leaving her. Charlotte could not imagine what could possibly compel a parent to leave their child. She could not imagine leaving George to someone else's care for so long, though she knew that many women of her station did just that.

Mary snorted at her own words and continued.

"I am nothing like a lady, of course, Lady Charlotte. I could not learn any more after he left. I do not think my aunt and uncle liked that I could read and write better than their children. I tried to listen to people after that. I wanted to be a lady, just as my father had wanted for me, so when my aunt sent me to the market to get food, I listened to how the ladies spoke, the ones I passed on the street. I did it for years. Day and night, I practiced so that I might sound like them. It made my aunt angry to hear me speak. She said I was trying to live above my station, 'puttin' on airs,' as she said, and that I was trying to be better than they were."

Charlotte tried to hide her surprise. Mary spoke very well for the most part. Yes, her accent was somewhat coarse and her inflection slightly off, but nothing so horrible that one could not overlook it. A few lessons with the right teacher and one might not even know that she had not been born into a genteel family. Charlotte wanted to ask Mary if her aunt had hurt her, but she was quite sure she already knew the answer, and to broach the question would do no good for her friend. Mary needed to get beyond that - she was never going back. She was moving forward and Charlotte was determined to help her.

"Would you like to learn more?"

Surprise lit Mary's face, as she smiled like sunshine. "Could I?"

Charlotte smiled in return. "Of course. I will teach you. Once dinner is over, we shall have our first lesson."

Mary looked admiringly at the book as if it was a grand treasure she had just unearthed.

"I have always wondered what stories and wisdom were hidden in books like this. Now, I shall be able to find out."

What kind of people did not allow a child to further their education?

"I will teach you everything I know, Mary. Languages, history, etiquette. Everything! So long as you are here, I shall be your tutor and I shall teach you."

"Will you? Truly?"

Charlotte took Mary's hand. Disappointment had colored Mary's view of everything, and kindness was hard for her to accept, but it would not deter Charlotte.

"Everything I know, you will know too. I can even enlist a professional if you wish it."

"No," Mary replied quickly. "I would be happy to learn from just you. I have watched you, just as I did those ladies when I went to market. I have been trying to learn from you too. I am sure I will be in good hands." She leaned forward, put her hand on Charlotte's arm, and gave it a little squeeze. "Thank you."

Charlotte could not understand her feelings as she placed her hand on Mary's to return the feelings. She was filled with both sadness and joy. She wanted to help, but the fact that her friend needed such aid was a source of pain to her.

"There is no need for thanks. I am pleased to do it."

Mary released her. "Then I shall wait until after

dinner. You should probably go. I expect that His Grace would not want you to be late."

Charlotte nodded and stood. *His Grace! What a funny child was Mary.*

"After dinner then."

She was met at the door by one of the maids.

"Lady Benton, Mr. Watts is here. So is Mr. Trundle."

Charlotte looked at the woman confused.

"Mr. Trundle? Who is he?"

"A guest of the duke's, I think."

Mary looked at her, curiosity reflected in her eyes. Charlotte felt uneasy. Who was this man and why had her father invited him to dinner?

"Thank you. I shall be down straight away. Could you ask Miss Lefebvre to meet me on the stairs?"

"Yes, Lady Benton."

Charlotte left the room and waited for Sophie. As she arrived, Sophie was full of questions. "Did the Duke say anything to you?" Sophie questioned as they descended the stairs.

"Not a word," said Charlotte. "I have no idea who this man is, or why my father would do such a thing as to invite him to dinner when he knew that James was invited. James will not relish the company of a stranger."

Sophie looked at her with concern.

"Something is not right."

Charlotte's heart quickened. Her father, James, and the unknown man were standing apart and awkwardly shifting from foot to foot in the entranceway as she reached the bottom of the stairs. William emerged from the study a moment later and joined them. Charlotte stopped at the bottom of the stairs and watched silently. What was her father up to?

She gripped the sides of her dress as anxiety threatened to unseat her composure.

No matter what Father is up to, you must remain of a clear mind. Perhaps there is nothing to this at all.

"Charlotte, I see you have finally decided to join us." He sounded almost jovial, but her father's declaration caused all eyes to turn in her and Sophie's direction. They approached the group.

"Good evening, Father," said Charlotte.

Her father immediately stepped forward, his hand on the shoulder of the man Charlotte presumed to be Mr. Trundle.

"Charlotte, may I present Mr. Samuel Trundle. He is the third son of Viscount Lindley. He has made quite a name for himself with his business investments in London. Samuel, this is my daughter, Lady Charlotte, Countess Benton."

Charlotte curtseyed as Sophie stood a few steps behind her. "Mr. Trundle."

"It is a great pleasure to meet you, Lady Benton. Your father has told me much about you."

She looked at her father. There was a sparkle in his eye. It made Charlotte nervous.

"The pleasure is all mine, Mr. Trundle. You are most welcome in our home."

Charlotte's gaze turned to James. She smiled and stepped toward him.

"And James, my dear. I am so very pleased to have you join us as well. I have been looking forward to it."

James' eyes remained on her as he answered. A smile tugged at his lips and made Charlotte's heart flutter. "So have I."

Her father cleared his throat. "Shall we have something to build the appetite? I believe I have some port in the drawing-room."

The members of the group nodded and followed her father and Mr. Trundle. The pair were talking amongst themselves and Charlotte could not quite hear what they were speaking about.

"Is not port usually drunk after dinner?" James questioned, as he leaned close to her to whisper in her ear.

"Usually," Charlotte replied. "But father has found it to be quite good in stimulating his appetite if taken before a meal. It is something he learned from the Duke of Compton, after ."

James smiled painfully. "I see. I have a lot to learn, it would seem."

Charlotte smiled. "Now that you are out more, I am sure you will become acquainted with many changes that have taken place of late."

"I should hope so. I would not want to embarrass you."

Charlotte looked at him calmly. "Oh James," she declared. "You could never embarrass me."

They entered the drawing-room and it wasn't long before her father was plying the men with port. Charlotte tried to stay close to James, wanting to speak with him, but her father insisted that she remain close to him instead, and help entertain Mr. Trundle.

"You make London sound quite alluring, Mr. Trundle. I wonder that you could bear to leave it." Charlotte sipped her drink and tried to be polite.

"I am afraid that the fresh air of the country is better for my constitution," he said modestly.

"Are you ill, Mr. Trundle?"

"Not at all, I assure you. My physicians have advised that if I wish to stay hale and healthy, then some fresh air from time-to-time would do me good. Industry in London has grown so much that the air is often filled with the residue of it. But I declare that there is no greater city in the world. The pleasures to be found there are not to be had anywhere else. I hope that I might see you there in the future."

Charlotte smiled modestly. "I thank you, Mr. Trundle, but I rarely have cause to go to London. I have visited it a handful of times, and, as you say, it is quite amazing, yet I find the comforts of the countryside far more rewarding."

"But Lady Benton, could you not see yourself dividing your time between country and city? Your presence would be much welcomed at court, or at the society parties in London, as I am sure it is welcomed here."

"I am not one to put my faith in society for company, Mr. Trundle. A few close friends are all I need." Charlotte glanced in James' direction. He sat with her brother and Sophie and looked quite amused. "And I already have that here."

"An enchanting lady, such as yourself, could never be in want of good company, I am sure. I hope that we can become much better acquainted and that, in time, I might be considered a part of your good company."

That was direct. Charlotte looked at her father's friend and tried to hide her surprise. "Anything is possible, Mr. Trundle."

He took her hand and kissed it. "Then I will endeavor to make it so."

Shock made her speechless at his brazen action. She barely knew him. Kissing her hand was too much. However, she noted that her father did not seem to mind. In fact, he seemed quite pleased.

He preened. "Shall we go in for dinner?" said her father, standing up and rocking back and forth on his heels in a self-satisfied way. "After all, that is why we are all here."

Charlotte suppressed a smile at her father's sudden urge to see them at the dinner table. Why the rush?

"Lead the way and we will follow, father," William declared.

Her brother was in bright spirits. Charlotte wondered what had caused him so much joy. She looked at James, but his expression seemed as baffled as she was. Whatever the reason, it would have to wait. Her father was already walking with Mr. Trundle into the dining room.

The meal was excellent, and the conversation lively, but everything stopped when her father suddenly drew their attention with the clinking of his fork against his wine glass.

"I say, everyone. I'm quite sure that you must be wondering why I have invited my esteemed colleague, Mr. Trundle, to join us this evening, despite his being a man none of you have met before."

Her father smiled, as did Mr. Trundle, but Charlotte felt instantly tense, her expression one of bafflement. She sat opposite the man, and the happy expression he presented did not calm her nerves at all. After he was so forward, she had decided she did not like him. He had stared most rudely at James throughout the meal, and Charlotte could feel her friend's discomfort from where he sat beside her.

"Please, Your Grace," said Mr. Trundle. "This is neither the time nor the place. Could this not wait until a little later?" He looked at Charlotte and grinned. "I am sure Lady Benton will want to discuss matters in private."

Charlotte's gaze turned to her brother, hoping he might be able to ease her confusion. What was Mr. Trundle talking about? But William looked as lost as she felt. He looked at her, his eyes like saucers, shaking his head subtly.

"Please, Mr. Trundle, what matter is this you are referring to?"

"You see?" said her father with a glint in his eye that was terribly uncharacteristic. "Charlotte is eager as well. Why wait? Happy news should always be shared."

Fear gripped her heart.

Happy news? What have you done, Father?

"Everyone, I am pleased to announce that Mr. Trundle has asked for Charlotte's hand in marriage, and, naturally, with no more worthy prospects, I have given my consent."

There were no words to describe the horror her father's declaration had elicited in her. How could he do such a terrible thing to her? Charlotte looked at James for help but found none. His expression was stoic as he looked intently at her father. William seemed likewise dumbfounded.

James' chair suddenly scraped across the floor as he got to his feet.

"This is wonderful news indeed. I wish I could stay to celebrate with you, but I fear that my ailing stepmother will be looking for me. I did not realize how late it had become."

Charlotte's jaw dropped, but she had no chance to reply as her father spoke immediately, rising from his seat.

"I am sure we all understand, James. Please, give Mr. and Mrs. Watts my best wishes. Let me see you to the door."

"Thank you, but no, your Grace. You have important guests and I would not consider tearing you away from them."

It was too much. Charlotte got to her feet. "Then I shall see you out. After all, you are *my* guest."

She left the table without another word, aching inside. She wanted to cry and scream at the same time - what did her father think he was doing, accepting a marriage proposal for her without even mentioning to her that someone had asked? Then to announce it in front of everyone as if he considered the matter settled when she had yet to utter a word. She was a widow, and had her majority – legally, he had no right to do this to her. But, obviously, he did not consider that a matter of concern at all.

It took all of her strength to hold herself together as she walked. She stopped in the hallway and turned to James. "I did not know of this. I have never met that man before today and I have *no* interest in marrying him. You must believe me."

The words jumped from her lips. She had to explain to him that she had no part in this, or he might think she had invited him there for the announcement, to humiliate him, when it was not the case.

"There is nothing to explain. I know your father well, Charlotte. I know you had nothing to do with this. You would never have invited me if you had. I know of Samuel Trundle from my father. He is very wealthy and well-connected, despite being only a third son. My father connected them after they met in London some months ago."

Angry tears stung her eyes as she listened. "My father has been planning this all along. He wanted me here to broker a deal? I am to be his bargaining chip?"

Her hands folded into fists at her sides.

James looked at her with the strangest expression. It was neither calm nor angry. It was more one of resignation.

"He will be a good match for you, Charlotte. He will be able to provide a good life for you and George."

Charlotte stepped toward him. Her words were firm. "I do not want this match for me or my son."

"I am afraid there is no way around it. Your father seems to have sealed the agreement."

Her father's voice suddenly interrupted them.

"You are still here, James? I came to check on Charlotte. It does not present a good impression when half of those present leave the table during the meal, especially with your fiancé present."

"Father..."

"Of course, your Grace. I am sorry to have kept Charlotte so long. If you both will excuse me, I need to return home as soon as possible."

James did not hesitate. His feet were moving away from them before the words were completely out of his mouth. Charlotte turned to stop him but her father took hold of her arm.

"Let him go," he growled.

Her head snapped in his direction. "We should *both* go."

Her father's grip tightened. His voice was low.

"Charlotte, he chose to go. I did not chase him. There is still a meal to enjoy and guests to entertain. You and Mr. Trundle will have a great deal to discuss and I will not have you embarrass me."

Charlotte shook her head in disbelief. "How could you do this, Father?"

He released her arm. "What I do is for the best."

"The best for who? You? Certainly not for me. I had no part of this. I am solely some sort of collateral to you, aren't I, father."

Her father's expression stilled. "We will discuss this later."

CHAPTER FIFTEEN

"Father, you have gone too far. What was the meaning of such a scene? Charlotte was speechless. I was stunned. Poor James was so uncomfortable he was forced to leave. I cannot imagine what Miss Lefebvre or Mr. Trundle thought. Why would you do such a thing?"

William's voice filled their father's office like thunder. Charlotte could not remember ever seeing him so impassioned. She was thankful for it. Her own emotions were so scattered and her nerves so tense that she was afraid of what she might say if her temper got the better of her.

Despite William's words, their father's expression remained unmoved.

"I do not understand your question, William. I cannot see what I have done wrong. Am I not duke? Is this not my household? Was that not my table?"

Her brother took a deep breath. "Yes. But..."

"And am I not Charlotte's father?"

"Yes."

"Then what wrong have I done? I have matched my

daughter with a more than suitable husband who can provide for her and her child. The match should be acceptable to all parties. It certainly is for Mr. Trundle." Her father turned to her. "He has done nothing but praise you since he first laid eyes on you."

"I cannot say the same for him," Charlotte retorted.

Her father's response was immediate. "Oh really? What fault do you find in him? I found none. He is a very agreeable man and far more attractive than his counterparts. Not to mention the fact that he is of noble birth, and one of the wealthier men in London. All of these things make him very suitable."

The words cracked over Charlotte like a whip. She was on her feet in an instant. "Have you no shame, father? You speak as if that is all there is to compatibility in marriage. You speak of me as though I were a prize hog. It's humiliating!"

The Duke looked at her, confused.

"What have I to be ashamed of? I am doing what fathers have done for centuries before me: making sure that the prosperity of my legacy remains intact. Marriage has always been a means of doing so and it will always be so, I imagine."

She could not believe her ears. "Father, you are doing this for yourself and no one else. You have never considered me, or William, in your actions."

Her father's face became grim.

"I do everything for my family. I do whatever is necessary, though I see that it is seldom appreciated."

"How can one appreciate not being included in decisions which involve one's life? No one could. You, more than anyone, know that feeling. You hate to be left out of the slightest of matters, far less something significant, yet you do not ever think that your children might feel the same way."

"I think my children should know their place and what is expected of them. This unladylike behavior is hardly what I raised you to present."

"I am sorry, father, but I do not think my honesty unladylike in the least." She took a deep breath. "My entire life you have commanded us rather than speak to us. Always orders and never instruction or kindness. You treat William like your replica and me as a tool. We are neither."

Charlotte's passions were rising. Her skin tingled, her heart pounded fiercely in her chest as her breath quickened with every word she uttered.

"You used me to gain access via my children to the Dornthorpe estate when you arranged my marriage to Malcolm, when you knew that I loved James."

Her father stood. "And were you not happy in that match?"

"Yes, I was. But you know how I felt. I loved James. I missed him. I was in mourning and yet you were already preparing to pass me off to another man."

"James was dead. What did it matter? You could not spend your entire life mourning him."

Charlotte's lips trembled with anger. "He is not dead now."

"Do not think I have not seen what is going on. I have noticed you seem to wish to renew your acquaintance on the same level it was, before James Watts left for war. I tell you now it will not do. He will not do. Not for you."

"Why not?"

"Have you seen the man? How could anyone wish him to be in their company? How many dinner tables would welcome such a sight with their soup? Even Mr. Trundle was disturbed to have him at dinner."

Charlotte's nostrils flared. "He stared at James the entire night. What sort of manners did that display? He was disturbed? He made James nothing but uncomfortable with the way he was looking at him."

"You cannot blame Samuel for that. I felt the same when I first saw James again."

William stepped forward.

"Father. Be reasonable."

"You cannot think that James Watts is in any way superior to Samuel Trundle."

Her father looked at him squarely.

Charlotte responded, even though her father had leveled the question at her brother. She could not allow her father to say such things and say nothing herself in response.

"I do, father. I think James far superior to *your* Mr. Trundle."

"I would agree," William stated. He moved to stand at her side. "I think you have crossed the line, Father. It was one thing to consider a marriage proposal and initially say nothing to Charlotte of it, but it is another entirely to agree to it, and then to announce it officially at a dinner party. You did all of this when you knew that James was invited to dinner this evening."

"What did it matter if he was invited or not. He would find out eventually. He could count it fortunate that he was one of the first to know."

Her father's retort set Charlotte's blood boiling. "You speak as if everything is agreed upon and this wedding is going to go forward. I tell you now that it will not."

The look of disbelief on her father's face was more than worth it. His brow knitted tightly.

"I beg your pardon?"

"I will not marry that man," Charlotte repeated clearly. She held her head high at her father's displeased gaze. "I married once before because you wished it. I accepted it then, but I will not now. Not again. I cannot."

"Charlotte, do I understand you correctly? You will refuse the match I have made for you."

Inside she trembled, but outside she appeared resolute. She had to. Her father would pounce on the slightest frailty. "Yes, Father, you understand correctly."

His jaw clenched and his eyes squinted to slits. "Am I to understand that you have *other* intentions for yourself and my grandson?"

"You are. And I will thank you to remember that your grandson is already the Earl of Benton, and will be, within the near future, the Marquess of Dornthorpe – and that I am his legal guardian, and am in charge of his inheritance until he reaches his majority. Your intentions for his estate will not come to pass without my say so."

Her father gaped at her for a moment, then completely ignored most of what she had said.

"If you are thinking that James Watts will be the man you shall marry, then I beg to inform you that you have miscalculated drastically. The war damaged him beyond repair. His mind is not what it was. You think I know nothing, but I know a great deal more than you. His father has told me of his nightmares. His strange behaviors. He cried out every night for months after his return."

She wanted to rebuff his words, but she had no evidence to the contrary. She knew nothing of James' nightmares or experiences during the war. In fact, she had never heard this before. James never wanted to talk about them and she had not pressed him for fear of driving him away.

Her father stepped out from behind his desk, his steps slow and methodical as he approached her. "You saw what he did tonight. As much as you may think him worthy, the man himself knows otherwise. He left here because he knew my arrangement was better for you and that he could not compete with a man such as Trundle." He faced her. "He will not marry you, Charlotte. He knows your connection with him would only bring you down in society. James has always cared for you. He would never do what he felt would be detrimental to you. It is his finest quality."

The merit of her father's words silenced her. James did care for her. She knew it, and because of it, he would more than likely behave as her father presumed. He had left that night had he not? He did not want her near him in the first place – he had said those words himself.

Her countenance fell at the thought. If James had the chance, would he deny their feelings and give her over as he already had done before? He could have come to her before when she was to marry Malcolm Tate, but he had watched her marry another man rather than subject her to the life he believed she would have with him.

But he was wrong then. He could be wrong now.

But how could she convince him otherwise? How could she make him see what she had always known about them? They were perfect for each other.

"I can see by your expression that you know what I say is true."

Her father looked at her sternly. Charlotte averted her gaze. She turned to William but her brother's face seemed to show that he believed her father's words as much as she did.

Charlotte lowered herself into a chair. She did not have the desire to stand nor to continue the conversation. Her heart was heavy. The evening had begun with such hope, but now all seemed lost. If James did not want her, if he chose instead to live his life alone, then could she remain a widow and raise her son alone? It was an unlikely venture, even with the resources of the Earldom of Benton at her disposal. Her son held a title. He would need a father's lead. Could she deny him a father because the man available to fill that role was not the man she loved?

Her brother stepped forward as a voice of reason. His tone no longer angry, but compassionate as he placed a hand on her shoulder.

"Charlotte should not have to choose between them. You do not know James' heart any more than we do. Perhaps he would marry her."

Their father's laugh tore away at Charlotte's resolve. He hardly ever laughed and it was disconcerting to hear it. "The day James Watts walks into my office and asks for Charlotte's hand will be the day I give it. However, I assure you it is a day that will never come. He did not come before the war and he will not come now. He knows he is even less suitable now than he was before. He has not the nerve."

Charlotte's lip trembled as she fought disappointed tears. James would never be unsuitable in her eyes. There was no one more suitable. He was the man who lived in her heart, had done so, even when she had thought him dead. How could she abandon her love for him when he lived? It was all too unfair.

"Your sister is no longer a child," her father went on directing his remarks to William. "She knows what is expected of a woman of her station. She can no longer live her life in fancy and whim, hoping for something which will never be. She is a respectable woman of position and title, with a son an Earl, and meant to become a Marquess. Do you think she can just sit forever and hope that another match will come to her?" Her father looked at her and Charlotte met his eye. "Your sister is no fool. She knows what is best, even if it is not what she wants. In this life, it is seldom that situations allow us to have what we want in life. It is the choices we make that propel us."

William contradicted him.

"You have not given Charlotte a choice."

"Fine. I will."

Charlotte looked her father in the eye as he asked the question she did not want to answer.

"Will you marry Samuel Trundle or will you not?"

Charlotte looked at her father.

"Give me time and I will answer you." She stood. "Right now, I have something more pressing to attend to."

Charlotte rose from her seat and strode to the door. She was not moved by her brother's shocked expression or by her father persistently calling her name. She would not answer now. She had to speak to James. But first, she had a lesson with Mary.

MARY COULD NOT HAVE BEEN MORE DELIGHTED when Charlotte found her. She seemed on the edge of the heavens at the prospect of their lesson.

She smiled at Charlotte.

"Are you ready for our lesson, Lady Charlotte?" she said, with a smile.

Charlotte forced a smile, her answer soft. "Yes. Yes, of course."

Unfortunately, her false smile did not fool Mary. "Something is wrong. Can you not teach me today?"

"No. Of course I can. That is why I came."

"Something happened at dinner. Was it that man the duke invited?"

They moved toward the window seat and sat. "Yes," Charlotte admitted. "My father wishes me to marry him."

Mary looked at her curiously. "You do not want to?"

Charlotte shook her head.

"Why?"

The weight of her father's desire and her own forced the truth from Charlotte's lips. "I love another."

The wide-eyed look Mary gave her made Charlotte chuckle. "You love someone else? Who?"

The smile betrayed her heart before the words left her lips.

"His name is James. James Watts."

"The man whom you invited to dinner this evening?"

"Yes. I have loved him my entire life."

Mary leaned closer. "How wonderful."

Had she looked like that when she was Mary's age? Wide-eyed and wondering? Charlotte remembered being besotted by the idea of love, but it was the first time she'd ever seen the expression on another.

"It is wonderful," Charlotte replied. She smiled brightly. "He is wonderful."

Mary sat back.

"But his Grace does not approve of him?"

Again, Charlotte shook her head.

"Whyever not?"

"My father has his ideas of what is right for me. They do not coincide with my own, so we are in conflict. However, never mind that. I have come to teach you, not to complain about my difficulties."

"You can complain. I like the fact that you talk to me. I have never had someone I could call a friend before."

"You do now." Charlotte took Mary's hand. "I have nursed you and watched you grow strong. I feel as if we are more than friends, but kin. Sisters."

Mary glowed at her words.

"I have always wanted siblings. Of my own... my cousins never treated me with any more respect than my aunt and uncle did."

"You have kin now. Family. As of today, I consider you my sister and no less." She looked at Mary carefully. "I think perhaps you think more of William than as a brother?"

Mary's lips parted silently. Charlotte closed her hands around Mary's hands. She needed to caution her. William had never indicated feeling more for Mary than as a ward. If her friend did have affection for him, it was better she put it aside. "My brother is not a man who plays with women's affections. If he felt something for you, he would tell you. He would make it clear."

"He would never look at one such as me. Not as a woman." Mary's gaze lowered. "But it does not mean that I cannot admire him. And I do admire him. I find him one of the best men I have ever met, and I am pleased to be in his acquaintance, if even for a short while."

Charlotte sighed gently. There was nothing wrong with affection; she only wished to protect her new friend from pain, for she knew, all too well, the pain of love unrequited. She feared William might be that for Mary.

"I think we are more alike than we think, you and I. We each have someone in our hearts who seems so far removed from us."

"Your Captain Watts is not so far removed from you, Lady Charlotte," Mary countered. "He came to dinner."

"And he left when my engagement was announced."

"What?"

The exclamation and Mary's expression were unforgettable. "But you said..."

"I do not wish to marry the man. My father has already agreed to it and I must give him an answer soon."

"What will you do?" Mary questioned.

"I must find out, once and for all, what James feels for me. I must know whether he will step forward to fight for what may be between us, or retreat and leave me to my fate with Mr. Trundle."

Mary looked confused. "Why must he be your fate?"

How could she explain a situation that Mary would never face herself? The choices which one with a title, and with a son destined for more, had to make.

"My son needs a father to mold him into the man he is to become. I can teach him, but I am no man to teach him a man's ways. George is already Earl of Benton – he will be confirmed into the title by the House of Lords once he is of age – but by then, it is most likely that he will be Marquess of Dornthorpe as well. I have to ensure he has everything he needs to be a man his father would be proud of. That means marrying and giving him a home with stability, love, and support."

"So, you must marry someone?"

"Yes," Charlotte answered woefully. "I have no choice. Whilst legally, as a widow, I might do otherwise, despite my father's wishes, I must consider what is best for my son, not only myself. I can no longer be selfish. I must consider his welfare above my own desires."

She could see the pity in Mary's eyes.

"That is a difficult situation to be in."

Charlotte smiled to reassure her.

"It is, but I already know my course. Whichever way things turn. I know where I must go."

CHAPTER SIXTEEN

The announcement of Charlotte's betrothal ate at
James like wolves on a carcass. The thought of her
marrying that man, whose eyes had constantly sought
him over dinner, looking at him with fascinated repul-
sion, was more than he could bear.

And the Duke of Mormont had been thorough in his
destruction of James' hopes. The man knew precisely
what it would do to James to hear that Charlotte was
intended for another, and what's more, what it would do
to him to hear it at the table, as a guest, when politeness
would force James to say nothing, to smile and accept it,
though it drove a knife into his heart. He would never
forget the look of satisfaction on the Duke's face as he had
made the declaration – he had been very pleased with
himself.

The invitations to Caldor House were incessant over
the following days. Charlotte kept asking him to call
upon her, but James refused to respond. He knew it
would only be a matter of time before she appeared at his

door. Perhaps that was the reason he refused to reply to her letters. He wanted her to come to Watton Hall - he wanted her to come to him. He sat in the parlor and waited.

It was late in the morning several days later when Betsy arrived looking for him. The young woman bowed her head and smiled at him politely.

"Master James, Lady Benton is here. Should I show her in?"

James stood, heart pounding, and with all the composure he could muster, spoke. She was there.

"Yes, see her in."

He paced back and forth as he waited for the maid to show Charlotte into the room. He had already planned his response to her expected queries about why he had refused to answer her invitations. He believed himself prepared to hear whatever she had to say, to face her unflinchingly and be strong. He would not waiver. He would prove himself the most admirable of men, the most honorable, by putting her before himself. What did it matter if he wanted her for himself? She had a better alternative. Was it not for the best that she take it?

Is it? You love her. Does Samuel Trundle, or does he merely see her title and her father's connections? Is he more suitable? Perhaps there is a better match. Perhaps...

"Master James. Lady Benton."

He turned at the sound of the maid's voice and was met by the brooding eyes he adored. Charlotte stood stoic – she did not smile or show any signs of merriment, as she usually would when they met.

She has made her decision and has come to tell me.

The thought came unbidden and was more painful than he could ever have imagined.

"Thank you. Please, leave us."

The maid looked at him skeptically but did as he asked. An unchaperoned lady alone with her master was hardly acceptable, even if that lady was a widow, and well-known to the house, but she knew better than to question him or imply impropriety.

His heart was still loud in his ears as he stepped towards Charlotte.

"I knew you would come."

"I had hoped not to have to. I hoped you would have come to me."

Her words were sad as she spoke, yet she moved towards him as if there were nothing between them.

They stood facing each other. A step separated them but much more stood between.

"I wish you all the happiness in the world, Charlotte. I can only pray that Mr. Trundle will endeavor to deserve you."

"Stop it."

The space between them disappeared and Charlotte's hands rested upon his cheeks. She had stolen his breath in an instant. The intensity in her eyes was intoxicating and he could not tear himself away. He did not want to.

He covered her hands with his.

"Charlotte, what are you doing?"

"What I have to, because I know you will not."

Her reply was both curious and confusing.

"What do you think I will not do?"

"Stop me from marrying Samuel Trundle."

Her response took him by surprise. It was not a scenario he had anticipated, and he had considered much in his days of avoidance.

"How can I, when he is your father's match for you."

"He is not mine." Charlotte's fingers traced the sides of his face, moving over the scars as if they were not there at all. "He could never be mine. How could I want such a man, when there is already someone else in my heart?"

Thunder rolled somewhere off in the distance. It felt like his heart pounding in his chest and it shook him just as profoundly. There was only one thing he wanted to know.

"Who is in your heart?" he said.

Her smile was slow in coming, but soon it radiated across Charlotte's face like the sun. "Whom do you think is in my heart, silly man? Who has always been in my heart?"

His hands slipped from hers. His arms felt heavy and his knees weak. "Perhaps I should not be."

Charlotte shook her head vehemently.

"Yes, you should be. What other place is there for you, but with me? James Watts, I have loved you my entire life. Since the day we met, there has never been anyone else who has occupied my heart so completely, so totally. I chose you then and I choose you now. I do not care what my father says. I will not let him sway me this time, nor will I allow you to do so. I love you, James. I love you with all my heart."

He had her love. It was all he had ever wanted. He took hold of her hands and removed them from his face.

"I do love you, too, Charlotte. I always have. But I cannot give you what you deserve. I do not have the means."

The words were leaden on his tongue and his mouth was filled with bile. He hated the truth, but yet he could not avoid it. She deserved everything, but he had nothing to give her. He did not even have employment.

"Samuel Trundle can afford to give you the best of everything. He will teach George about business and investments, and give you an enviable home with everything your heart desires."

"I have already had those things. One thing was missing."

The conversation was tearing him apart inside. He should have stopped it, but instead, he continued.

"And what was that?"

"Me. I could not be myself in it. I had to be what everyone else expected. I had to be what was desirable. Not myself. You have never asked me to be anything but myself." She breathed deeply, her eyes downcast as he watched her trembling lips.

"What is it, Charlotte?"

"My father said you would do this." She turned her back on him, her voice breaking as she spoke. "He said you would do what is right for me, that you would not return my love. You would not want to marry me. He said you would never do it because you knew you were not right for me. You are less suitable now than before, he said." She laughed bitterly. "Do you know what he said? He said he would agree to our marriage if you only came to his office and asked. William heard him so declare, as did I. Do you know why he said so? Because he knew you would never do it. I did not want to believe it. I hoped... I do not know what I hoped." It seemed that she was about to begin weeping.

James stepped closer, the pain in her words constricting his heart.

"My father demands an answer," she went on. "He wants me to accept Mr. Trundle and marry him without question. I cannot do it. He demanded, but I could not agree. I came here to tell you how I feel. I was determined not to give in to you again, determined to wait until you came to me, until you admitted your feelings to me, but I had to come finally. You always win against me. I suppose this is another victory for you, but I had to come. I had to say how I felt, even if you did not feel the same."

"But Charlotte, I do feel the same."

She turned to him with tear-drenched eyes which filled him with guilt and shame.

"I see. But not enough to step forward with me. Not enough to love me past your fears." She waited but he could not speak. "I must go."

She was brave enough to come to him and say what was in her heart, yet he had not the courage to do the same himself. He was forcing her to take the risk, while he stood by in silence, denying her what she wanted. Denying himself what he needed. He needed Charlotte.

James watched her walk away, and he felt as if he was losing himself again. The light was leaving his life and only darkness would follow. He could not go back to the dark. He could not go back to his solitary existence. He could not go back to a life without her.

Before he could think, he was moving. He crossed the room at almost a run, wrapping his arms around Charlotte to keep her from escaping. She sucked in a surprised breath, but James only held her tighter.

"Do not go."

"Why not? Why should I stay? My son needs a father, James. My father has found a man who wants to take on that responsibility and marry me. Everything says that I should agree. Yet I cannot. But I have no other options, do I? Who else wants me?"

"I do." He inhaled the sweet smell of her hair and revelled in the warmth of her slender frame where it rested against him. "I more than want you. I need you, Charlotte."

"Not enough."

"Too much." Neither good-sense nor fear could stop his heart from spilling the truth from his lips. He had to tell her what was in his heart before he lost her forever. He had to take the chance he had never taken before. He turned her in his arms to face him. Gritting his teeth, he tried to pace himself, lest he spill too many words, too many feelings, into incoherent speech. He needed to be clear. "Charlotte, I should let you go, but I simply cannot. I thought I could. I thought, that because I had watched you marry another before, I could do it again. But I cannot. This woke me up, Charlotte, and I cannot fall asleep again. I cannot see you with that man. I refuse to. Do you hear me? I refuse."

Tears rolled down her tender cheeks in streams, turning the rims of her eyes red.

"Then what will you do? How can you stop it?"

"You are my very breath, my very beating heart. I cannot be parted from you. Never." He stepped closer, love spurring him on as never before. "Knowing that you love me is enough to help me face any foe, any obstacle."

Charlotte trembled in his arms, evoking a need to hold her even closer and comfort her. Instead, he expressed his love in the only way that could, that he had never before risked. Heart racing, skin hot, ears filled with the sound of his heart, James brought his lips to meet Charlotte's. Tender at first, and then more passionate, he kissed her as if he needed her breath to keep him alive. When they parted, they were both breathless.

"James?"

He smiled boldly. "I have wanted to kiss you since I was a boy. And, I daresay, it was far better even than I imagined." He brushed a wisp of curls from her face and tucked them behind her ear. "Would you marry me, Charlotte? Would you devote your life to only me? If you will, I would do anything for you. I would walk across deserts and fight armies again, just to know that you would be there when I returned."

Charlotte wrapped her arms around him, resting her head on his chest.

"I have wanted nothing more in life than to be your wife."

"Then it is time I stopped our torture. I did not before. I will now. I concede to you, Charlotte. You win. You win it all. Everything I have I give to you. Though it is only myself, it is my all."

She squeezed him tight, her voice only a whisper against his waistcoat.

"Then I accept all of you, and give you all of me in return."

He could take it no longer. He lowered his head and lifted hers with a crooked finger.

"My love for you will never fail."

He pressed his lips to hers, breathing her in as her lips pressed tenderly against his.

I will love you forever.

CHAPTER SEVENTEEN

The days that followed their confession were more joyful than any before. James found himself lost in Charlotte's presence, reveling in having her near, and in the promises they'd made to each other. Now, it was time to act on them.

He arrived at Caldor House early that morning. His heart was beating steadily, but the sight of Charlotte descending the stairs soon changed that. Ignited by her presence, the even beat quickened immediately.

She was a radiant sight. Dressed in lavender and simple pearl jewelry, she was the epitome of understated beauty and elegance. Charlotte had never needed any extra adornments to make her beautiful, for she held a special beauty all her own. It was evident now more than ever.

James met her in the entranceway, and taking her hand, he bowed and kissed it. "You look lovely."

"Thank you."

Charlotte smiled, her cheeks turning a rosy hue. Her

eyes were bright and cheerful. He wove his fingers through hers.

"Are you ready?" Charlotte's nod made his heart beat faster. "Is your father here?"

"He is in his study."

"Hard at work, no doubt."

"Mr. Trundle visited him yesterday afternoon. He was with him for a very long time."

Charlotte's head bowed. She was anxious.

James tightened his hold on her hand.

"You need not worry yourself with his visit. He and your father can have each other for company. I will keep you for myself."

He started toward the study. His heart thundered, echoing the storm within him. He was going to face down the hardest man he'd ever met. You did not trifle with the Duke of Mormont; for he never backed down when challenged. He was used to winning - James had never known anyone like him. Today, he would face him for his daughter's hand.

They arrived at the door and James was almost deaf from the beating of his own heart. He raised his hand and knocked firmly on the solid door, much louder than he had intended.

The duke's voice sounded from inside. "Come."

Charlotte's breath hitched audibly. James turned to reassure her.

"You do not need to worry. You need say nothing. I will deal with this myself."

"Are you sure?"

"Of course. You have taken the boldest step. It is time for me to take the remainder."

He took hold of the door handle and took a deep breath before opening it.

The duke's study was immaculate, as always. He was seated behind the large desk, leaning back, his hands folded on the desk before him, as he watched them enter the room. His eyes became fixed on their joined hands and James could see the displeasure in his expression.

The duke stood slowly and bowed. A minimal bow, but more courtesy than James had expected.

"James, what brings you here?"

James smiled as he returned the greeting.

"I have a matter of great importance which I need to discuss with you, your Grace."

Again, the duke's eyes drifted to where James' hand joined with Charlotte's. James refused to release it. Instead, he kept his eyes on the man before him. Intimidation would not work on him today.

The duke chuckled. "You seem so grave. Please, have a seat. I take it that Charlotte will be remaining with us?"

"She will."

James did not allow the duke's apparent mirth to fool him. He knew the man too well to be persuaded that he was pleased with anything he saw.

They sat opposite each other, staring at one another in silent intensity, waiting for who would speak first – it was, he thought, childish, almost laughable. James decided it would have to be him - he would not allow Charlotte's father to lead him by the nose, indeed, James was determined to lead.

"Your Grace, we have known each other for many years. You have been one of my father's greatest clients, and your family, our closest friends. We have been joined in many ways, but today, I wish to propose the joining of our families on more intimate terms."

The Duke stiffened. "And what intimate terms do you speak of?"

"I have known your daughter for most of my life. You know of the fondness we shared as children. I am here to tell you that fondness has grown to something infinitely more. I love her."

"I see."

James turned to Charlotte. The love of his life was smiling at him brightly.

"I have asked her to marry me and she has accepted."

The duke scoffed.

"Rubbish," he exclaimed. "I do not see how that can be. You were here. You know I intend for my daughter to marry Samuel Trundle. What right have you to interfere in an already established arrangement?"

James' jaw clenched. "With all due respect, your Grace. What right have you to make arrangements when you have not even consulted your daughter? Charlotte is a grown woman. She has been married and has a child. As a widow, and of her majority, she is no longer under your thumb. She is free to make her own decisions, as well you know."

"She is also under my roof, under my protection. I am her father and I shall decide what is best for her."

These words angered James. The duke, it was evident, cared nothing for Charlotte's welfare, or that of her son; his primary concern was his business dealings with Samuel Trundle. That was why he had suggested that Charlotte return to Caldor House in the first place. That was why he had brought that man there to meet her.

"I am sorry, your Grace, but Charlotte has made her own decision. And she wishes to marry me."

The duke's gaze shifted from him to Charlotte.

"Is that so? Have you decided to go against my wishes?"

Charlotte met her father's gaze boldly. "I have, Father. I want to marry James. I will not marry Mr. Trundle."

The duke did not reply. He turned to James. "And you think that you can care for my daughter and grandchild? You do not have employment. How do you propose to feed them?"

"My father has given me a position within his practice."

The Duke was visibly incredulous. "You are no lawyer."

"No, I am not. However, I am a man with experience of business and one business is much as another is, in its basic requirements. I will manage his affairs and investments. I also have other prospects which I am entertaining. I do not see being able to care for my wife as an issue. And my father assures me that Lady Charlotte's dower rights are, unusually, not affected should she choose to remarry."

"And what of her social standing? Can you maintain the society to which she is accustomed? To which her son must become accustomed as he grows? You cannot tell me that you can, when we both know that you cannot. You have hidden yourself these many years, and for good reason. Did those reasons suddenly disappear? I cannot see that they have."

James' muscles tensed with the strain of holding in his temper. He was not oblivious to the duke's meaning. The man was goading him, trying to force him to see the faults in their union. The duke was too late. James had already faced those demons, many times over, before coming to ask for Charlotte's hand.

He smiled. "Thankfully, Charlotte and I agree we prefer the company of true friends over any broader society. The company of each other's family is enough for us."

The Duke's expression darkened as his neck turned crimson. "Is that so? And what if that company is no longer available."

"Then," said Charlotte. "We will be happy to be together and find other company."

There was confidence in Charlotte's words as she spoke. James turned to her with pride. She would not let her father sway her.

Nor will I.

"We can have our own family. Is that not right, Charlotte? You, George, and I. We can be all the company we need."

He could feel the Duke's ire but refused to look at him.

Charlotte turned to James with a grin.

"And whatever other children the Lord blesses us with."

The duke stood abruptly. "Enough," he declared loudly. "I will no longer participate in this charade. Charlotte is my daughter and I shall give her to whom I choose, and my choice is Samuel Trundle. If she will not do as I ask, then she is no longer any family of mine. I will disown her entirely. Do you hear me?"

James was on his feet in seconds. He stepped between Charlotte and her father protectively.

"I am sorry you feel that way, your Grace."

Charlotte clutched his hand as she stood beside him.

"So am I, Father. I suppose that today will be our last as a family. You need not trouble yourself with George nor with me. We will be well cared for elsewhere. You will never need to see us again. I have the full resources of the Benton Earldom to draw upon to take care of George's upkeep, as well as James – I will not need anything from you."

"Whether you approve of our union or not is irrelevant, your Grace." James said calmly."We have decided that our future is together. We will not change our minds no matter what you threaten." He looked at the duke coolly. "We will leave you now."

James offered his arm, and Charlotte entwined hers with it. He turned from the desk and led her toward the door.

The duke's voice resounded behind them. "You will regret this."

James stopped. He turned to the duke, Charlotte still on

his arm. "No, I believe it is you who will regret it. You will realize what it is to have no one, just as I did. You will lose your daughter and grandson. How soon after, will William turn away from you for what you have done to his sister? Not to mention how society will view your ex-communication of your daughter from your life because she chose to marry me. There are many, as I have learned recently, who still regard me as amongst their friends, and despite my marred appearance, they have welcomed me warmly."

The duke looked at him in silent defiance. "I am simply doing what is best for my daughter. You cannot tell me that you believe yourself Samuel Trundle's equal."

"I know I am not."

"You see, Charlotte. He admits it."

The duke's words were full of gratification as if such an admission was something to find pride in. James felt sorry for the man. His pride and arrogance would leave him very lonely in his later years if he was not careful.

"Happiness is not solely dependent on means, your Grace. It is about the connection of one spirit to another. Like minds make better companions than those brought together for personal advancement or profit. I will love your daughter more than a thousand Samuel Trundles ever could."

He looked at Charlotte tenderly. Her eyes were red and James could see the sorrow in her expression. Though she had expected her father to reject their union, the manner of it was perhaps more than she had expected it to be.

"You cause your daughter pain, your Grace, yet you

seem unaffected by it." James turned to the man who wished to stand between him and his happiness. "You break her heart with your refusals and threats. She loves you. Though I have never heard you say it, I believe you love her too, and yet you put your desires above hers. You put the needs of the Duchy above your daughter's heart and soul. She has never had a mother. You are her only parent, yet you would so easily forget her as your child rather than accept her choice?"

James was stunned, for the duke seemed speechless. He could not stop now. He might not be able to convince the man to accept him and bless the union, but he could finally tell him precisely what he thought of him.

"You chose for her before, and she accepted it. Has she not paid enough? Can she not find her own happiness now? I have always shown you respect, even though I disagree with how you treat your children. I kept my tongue for Charlotte's sake. I would have married her a long time ago, but war called me away and I wanted to protect the interests of this country. *Your* interests. Yet, for my efforts and pain, you reject me because of appearance."

The anger he felt was like a steady fire in his breast that kept him going. He expressed what he'd felt for the many years since his return - it was what he felt toward everyone who had once seen him as a man, but then as less because of the scars he bore.

"You said that I would not come to you, to ask for your daughter's hand. You believed me a coward who would not face you, so you set a parameter that you believed was insurmountable. You said you would agree to our union if I came here, to your study, and asked for your daughter's hand. I am here, your Grace, and yet you refuse to keep to the words you spoke. You demonstrate, in that, that you are no longer a man of honor, in any way. Instead, you reject us and turn your back on your only daughter. I feel sorry for you, your Grace. Today, you have lost the greatest treasure in your life. I hope one day you might see that."

He turned without another word of farewell. Charlotte's tears stained her cheeks and it hurt him to see it, but she smiled at him and took his arm again. He took hold of the handle of the door and turned it.

"I did say that." The duke's voice was low, almost soft compared to the ferocity with which he had spoken before. "I may be many things, but I am a man of my word. Charlotte, I did say that you could marry him if he came to me."

Charlotte turned to her father sharply. Her lips quivered but no words escaped them. James followed her gaze.

"I cannot change your mind," he continued. "I cannot change mine. I think that this is a mistake, but you have made your choice, and James has come to see it through. I cannot deny my own words. My word is my word and I must keep it. I am, James Watts, a man of honor, no matter what you think of me." The duke looked at him, defeated. "And so, I give you my blessing. You may marry my daughter."

CHAPTER EIGHTEEN

Charlotte was elated. The world was spinning in entirely new directions and she adored it. Her father had blessed their marriage, William was thrilled by the prospect of his sister and friend becoming as one, and today they were informing James' parents of their pending nuptials. There could be nothing better.

The sun shone down on Watton Hall and reflected the bright center of which James was in her life. George was with him, playing amidst the bushes of the garden as Charlotte reclined on the chaise beside Mrs Watts. Mr. Watts sat on a chair nearby reading his paper.

Mrs Watts was well again. She smiled brightly, her cheeks full and her eyes bright. The luster of her hair was slowly returning, and Charlotte anticipated that any day now, she would be completely her old self again. She turned to Charlotte with a smile.

"We are so happy you came today."

Charlotte smiled in return.

"As am I."

She could not wait to tell them, but James had said that he wanted it to be special. She had acceded. She wanted it to be special as well; for she knew that the Watts would celebrate their marriage where her father had only accepted it.

One of the maids rushed toward them.

"Mr. Watts, there are two young people here to see you. The Marquess of Cott and a young lady, sir."

John looked up from his newspaper.

"By all means, show them in, Betsy."

The woman turned and rushed back inside to retrieve her brother and his company. Charlotte already knew who was with him. Since her strength had returned fully, Mary and William were frequently in each other's company.

It would soon be time for Mary to leave them. James believed he had located her father in London, and they only awaited confirmation of his location and situation.

Mrs Watts turned to her.

"I did not expect William to call - and he brings company. How delightful. We shall have a full house again, just as it was when you were young."

Charlotte was pleased to hear the joy in her former governess's voice. Soon, everything would be as it was.

Better.

William was strolling down the steps from the terrace toward them when Charlotte turned around. Mary walked beside him. She looked so much better - a ribbon adorned her delicately curled hair, making the once limp strands look full and radiant, its dark gold color was like a field of ripe wheat. Her figure was still slender, but she was no longer gaunt.

"Hello, John. Hello Mrs. Watts."

Her brother bowed deeply as he greeted them. Mary stood quietly by his side. Her fingers fidgeted as she waited for an introduction.

"William." Mrs Watts smiled as she said his name, the delight echoing in her tone. "I am so pleased to see you."

She attempted to stand but William stopped her.

"There is no need to stand on my account. You seem quite relaxed where you are. I would not dare disturb you." He smiled and turned to Mary. "May I present Miss Mary Durand?"

Charlotte felt like a proud mother watching Mary presented to the Watts. She was a pretty girl and looked prettier still in her new day dress.

John Watts stepped forward as Mary curtseyed deeply.

"Good day to you, Mr. Watts. Mrs. Watts."

"Miss Durand, what a pleasure it is to finally meet you." Mr. Watts bowed to the young woman. He smiled at her pleasantly. "I am glad that William has finally seen fit to bring you to meet us, and that your health is fully restored."

"Thank you, Mr. Watts. I have greatly appreciated your kindness and wanted to convey my thanks personally. Lord William allowed me to accompany him today so that I might do so before I leave."

The words that slipped effortlessly from Mary's lips doubled Charlotte's pride. Mary's actions and manner reflected her efforts to learn during their time together. Her coarse tone was gone and her inflection was perfect. She was genteel, the very image of the lady she wished to be. She was a diamond in the rough that had simply needed a good polish. There was still more to do concerning her education, but Charlotte was sure that Mary was proud of what she'd accomplished thus far.

Despite her momentary focus on the vision which Mary presented, her brother's words soon sank in. She sat up quickly.

"Leave?"

George chortled as James plucked him into the air and approached them.

"Did I hear you say that you are leaving?"

William spoke up.

"Yes. I received confirmation this morning. Peter Durand has been located and is sailing for Tilbury Docks as we speak. Mary is to join him in London as soon as possible. I am taking her there myself. Her belongings are packed in the carriage. Miss Lefebvre has agreed to accompany us, for propriety's sake." He turned to the young woman. "It seems that our time with dear Miss Durand is nearing an end."

In the time since Mary arrived, Charlotte had made sure that she was outfitted appropriately. She now had new dresses and shoes to suit every occasion. Mary had been reluctant to accept them at first but had eventually acceded to the kind gesture. She had wanted to pay for them, but Charlotte had refused the offer. The girl had to learn to accept kindness without feeling compelled to immediately repay it. Charlotte was pleased to say she was now more willing to accept help, though not entirely comfortable with that yet.

Mrs Watts stood and Charlotte joined her. "To think that we are only meeting you now, when you must leave. I would have so wished to know you better, Miss Durand. I hope you will return to this county in the future so that we may become better acquainted."

A shy smile made Mary's cheeks red.

"I would like that." She raised her eyes to William. "If I receive an invitation I will surely come."

"Then consider yourself invited." Her brother's eyes twinkled with pleasure. "I will want to know how you progress in a city like London. I will not be a stranger and I hope that you will not be one either."

"I share your sentiments."

James stepped forward with George sitting upon his shoulders, holding onto his hair for security. Her son laughed merrily from his high perch.

"You will always be welcome in Alnerton, Mary." Charlotte took her friend's hands. "I shall miss you. Having you with us has been like having a sister."

Mary's blush deepened. "I feel the same, Charlotte. I have never had siblings, but I have always wanted a sister. Knowing you has been the nearest thing I have ever had to one."

William stepped between them and, looking from Charlotte to Mary, he smiled. "Then it is settled. We shall not part ways from our new friend." He turned to James. "Do you agree?"

"Wholeheartedly."

James made a face as George tugged on his hair.

William clapped his hands enthusiastically.

"Well, that is done. We must be on our way. I am sorry I did not bring Mary to see you sooner. It was very remiss of me."

Mr. Watts dismissed his apology with a gentle wave. "Think nothing of it. What thought do young people have for the old, when they have such pretty company to distract them?"

The compliment threatened to turn Mary scarlet. William simply smiled at her. "Miss Durand. Shall we go? Sophie awaits us in the carriage."

Mary nodded, her cheeks still flushed. "Very well."

"Good day to you all."

William offered his arm to Mary. She hesitated momentarily before placing her hand on it. She then nodded politely but did not speak further as they turned and left.

There was silence for a little while, then Beatrice spoke.

"She is quite shy, isn't she?"

Mrs Watts' comment startled Charlotte, who was lost in thought, wondering whether Mary still admired her brother and if he felt the same. She had to admit that, standing beside one another, they made a handsome pair.

"Her life has been a constrained and isolated one. Deprived of so much, she is still to blossom." Charlotte turned to Mrs Watts and smiled. "I look forward to seeing that day."

James wrapped an arm around her shoulders.

"So do I."

They moved back into the house as the sun reached its apex, seeking the refreshments which awaited them in the parlor. Mrs. White saw to George's lunch and his nap.

They sipped their lemonade and laughed as they spoke of what fun there was to be had in the coming winter. Christmas was a particular favorite time of the year for all of them, and Mrs Watts was most eager for it, as illness had spoiled her last Christmas.

"This year I will make up for it." Mrs Watts laughed and sipped her lemonade. "I shall make it a Christmas that will never be forgotten."

"Indeed."

James stepped through the door. Charlotte had not noticed him leave. She looked at him curiously. He had slipped out so quietly.

"Where were you?"

"There was something special I needed to collect."

Charlotte frowned.

"Collect?"

James stepped towards her.

"Yes. Something very special indeed."

Charlotte's heart faltered in her chest. Her mind reeled as she gasped, for James was no longer standing, but was, instead, on one knee before her, an ornate ring in his hand.

"Your grandmother's ring."

Charlotte looked at Mrs Watts. The ring, which once lived on her finger – given to her by John when they had gotten engaged - was no longer there. Another elegant one had replaced it. Mrs Watts squealed with delight as their eyes met in understanding and Mr Watts came to stand beside her. He placed a calming hand on her shoulder as he looked on with a proud smile. James witnessed neither reaction, for his eyes were only on Charlotte.

"Charlotte, I have already asked and you have already accepted, but it would never be right if I did not do it this way, with this ring." He gently took her hand and slipped the ring onto her finger as he continued. "Marry me, Charlotte. Make me the happiest man alive. I swear that I will make you happy all of my days. As long as there is breath in my lungs, I will love you."

Tears rolled down her cheeks uncontrollably. Her body shook as joy overtook her. She pulled him to his feet and flung her arms around James' neck as she sobbed.

"Yes. A thousand times yes."

She clutched him tightly, unable to move. He was her anchor, holding her to the earth as her entire being took flight. Through tears that blurred her vision, Charlotte looked at the ring on her hand. It was an antique setting, an heirloom passed down from generation to generation. She had thought that their visit today was a surprise. But now, Charlotte was the one who was surprised.

The pair embraced as Mr. and Mrs. Watts joined them to give their congratulations. The celebration was only the beginning; soon the entire house knew the news and all of the staff came to congratulate them.

Charlotte could hardly believe it as, one-by-one, the staff came and shook James' hand. No one grimaced at his appearance or shied away from him; instead, they earnestly congratulated him and shared their joy. She had never thought that such a thing would happen, yet now that it had, Charlotte could not imagine anything more wonderful. It was the perfect beginning for their new lives together.

CHAPTER NINETEEN

Six months later

She felt as if fire were covering her body. She could not keep calm. Her cheeks and neck were crimson, her nerves on delightful edge. She closed her eyes, hoping that the act would aid in relaxing her, but it was of no use. She fidgeted on the bench as Sophie and Mrs Watts did her hair.

"Calm yourself, my dear. It will be over soon enough."

Mrs Watts' sweet voice reflected her joy. She placed a gentle hand on Charlotte's shoulder, offering much-needed comfort. Charlotte placed her hand atop it, then opened her eyes and looked at her governess's reflection in the mirror.

"It feels as though I have waited a lifetime for this day."

"We all have." Mrs Watts smiled at her brightly. She continued to set pearl-covered pins into Charlotte's hair. "I will take this moment to admit that I have always wished for this day. Since you were children, I have hoped that one day you and James would become husband and wife, no matter the difference in your stations. Now that this day is here, I could not be more delighted."

"You have desired this for so long?"

Charlotte could hardly believe it, for her governess had never said a word on the matter, but she supposed she had always known it in her heart. They had always been so close.

Sophie smiled at her. Her large grin made her even prettier than usual.

"We shall make you a beautiful bride, Charlotte. Do not worry. We have made sure that everything will be perfect today. It will be a day you shall always remember."

"Indeed." Beatrice nodded in agreement. "We have everything prepared. You need not fret. Everything is already in place and nothing will go amiss."

"Absolutely not." Sophie chimed in as if on cue. "There. Your hair is finished. We need to get you dressed. It is almost time for the ceremony to start."

Mrs Watts looked surprised. She had come to check on Charlotte, but instead, had stayed far longer than she'd planned, talking.

"Yes. I must get back downstairs to greet the guests. I left William and John alone - who knows what they might have done?"

With a soft chuckle, the older woman left Charlotte to finish getting ready. Charlotte rose from the chair and turned.

The gown lay across the bed, a beautiful fall of the finest lace and silk. It was ivory in color and embroidered along the hem, neck, and sleeves in silver thread and glittering tiny gems, with an outer layer of fine translucent netting, also scattered with tiny sparkling gems. Her shoes were simple white satin slippers.

"You have such exquisite taste, Charlotte," said Sophie. "Every time I look at this dress, I wish it were my own wedding day."

Sophie helped Charlotte slip into the gown.

Charlotte smiled. "One day soon, it will be your turn, and I will be the one helping you prepare."

"I pray for it."

"Believe it will happen. I had to wait a long time for this day, but it has finally come. Yours will also. Just wait. One day, a man of worth will find you, and desire you for his own."

Sophie's cheeks rose in a smile. "I shall await that day."

The wedding party was a small one. James and Charlotte's intertwined hearts had made wedding preparation easy, for they agreed on everything, which was a good sign for the future, to Charlotte's mind. They had chosen not to have a large number of guests, nor anything excessively elaborate. They simply wanted to celebrate with those closest to them, and had chosen to have the ceremony at Watton Hall.

Sophie followed her out of the guestroom of Watton Hall, and her father met them on the stairs.

He was dressed in simple black, with a crisp white cravat, fixed in place by a jewelled pin. His hair was in the latest style, and the shine on his shoes rivalled that of his oiled hair. He was a striking sight for a man who was there out of obligation and not because he fully supported them. Charlotte appreciated it nonetheless.

"Father."

He looked at her as if she was a precious treasure he had never seen before. "Charlotte," he gasped. "You look radiant."

She blushed. "Thank you, Father."

She placed her hand on top of his as he extended his arm.

"Everyone is in place. They await your arrival," said the duke.

"Thank you for doing this, Father. I know you do not fully support this marriage, but I assure you that you will not regret your decision to bless our union." She smiled brightly, hoping he would understand. "We love each other more than anything. Life without this union would be unbearable to me."

Her father nodded stiffly. "I shall lead you to your betrothed."

They walked from the house, and the aroma of the wedding breakfast being prepared filled her senses and made her stomach rumble.

"You know, Charlotte," said her father, with a wry grin. "It is still not too late to change your mind."

Charlotte looked momentarily shocked until she saw

the smile on her father's face. "Naughty!" she said, laughing at his unexpected joke.

She was so excited that she had not been able to eat anything that morning, and was feeling the repercussions of it now. It would have to wait until later.

The sun's rays shone down like beams of light from heaven to bless her special day. They walked into the carriage and were conveyed the short distance to the Alnerton Village Church.

Inside the church, flowers decorated every pew, and garlands caught the light from the stained-glass windows. There were no more than twenty-five people present, but that was more than enough in Charlotte's mind. The vicar stood at the altar, with James and her brother waiting before him.

James turned to look, as the whisper of guests indicated her arrival. Charlotte lingered in the doorway a moment, her heart full and her feet immobile as James' eyes met hers. The world melted away at his smile and Charlotte felt sure that, in all of her life, no man had ever looked at her with such love. She smiled at him, her heart skipping in her chest.

Her father patted her hand. "Come, Charlotte. Everyone is waiting."

Snapped from her daze by her father's words, Charlotte followed him as he led her down the aisle towards her soon to be husband.

She could hardly hear the minister's words as he spoke. Her heart beat like drums at a march and her spirit felt so light that it seemed as if it was only James' hand holding hers which kept her tethered to the earth. She barely managed to answer when called upon.

"I do."

Their vows exchanged, and their union declared before an applauding gathering, Charlotte stood at her husband's side, her cheeks hurting from smiling so much. They paused on the steps of the church, the morning sun warming their faces, and James held her hand firmly, a grin on his face which lit up his countenance and made him more handsome in her eyes. He turned to her and placed a chaste kiss upon her lips to glorious uproar from the pleased onlookers.

"I love you, Charlotte."

"I love you too, James."

James stroked her cheek gently, then led her to the carriage, which quickly returned them to Watton Hall, where the wedding breakfast awaited.

For a short while, they were alone, then the guests descended upon the hall, emerging from their carriages, and hurrying inside. The folding doors between the two parlors had been opened, for the first time that James could remember, and tables laden with food were set along one wall, with smaller tables placed about the room.

Everyone settled to eating, drinking, and celebrating. Neither Charlotte nor James could stop smiling, for their joy was overwhelming and had been so long in coming that there was no containing it. Charlotte had no desire to hide her feelings. She was glad that James did not want to either.

They dined on the best fare available. Her father might not be fully behind them, but he would never have allowed her wedding breakfast to be less than opulently imposing, to demonstrate his wealth and influence. He had tried to persuade them to have the wedding breakfast at Caldor House but neither Charlotte nor James had desired it. They had wanted a simpler setting, for, if they had allowed him to, her father would have turned their wedding into a circus. John and Beatrice had kept it as they wished.

After some time, the servants moved the remaining food onto side tables, and one end of the room was cleared for dancing, with the small group orchestra tucked into one corner of the space. When the dancing began, Charlotte could not take her eyes from James, nor he from her. They danced around the room in each other's arms, their bodies in perfect alignment as if they had one mind governing them. She caught sight of her son in the arms of his nurse. George was smiling brightly and clapping as he watched them. This moment was all that Charlotte had ever wanted.

As the dance came to an end, they slowed and moved to where the doors onto the terrace stood open. Slipping through, they stopped, looking out across the gardens. James pulled Charlotte into his arms, and she rested her head on his chest. Her voice was barely a whisper when she spoke.

"I will love you forever."

"I am glad, for I thoroughly intend to do the same to you, *my wife.*"

There was a note of laughter in James' voice. The words sent a reverberation through Charlotte which permeated her bones and filled her heart to overflowing. She looked up to find her husband smiling down at her.

"You are finally my husband. We will be a family at last."

She raised her chin as her husband lowered his head to hers. Their lips met in a kiss that was more intoxicating than any wine, and Charlotte allowed herself to become drunk on the sensation of it. All thought of anything else departed her mind.

The man she loved was finally her husband. Now, it seemed to her, everything wrong had been made right and their lives would only get better because they had each other to rely on, come what may. There was no greater joy in the world.

SNEAK PEEK OF THE
ROGUE'S FLOWER

"Elsbeth?"

Miss Elsbeth Blakely, daughter to some unknown persons and nothing more than an orphan, turned her head to see Miss Skelton enter the room, her thin figure and skeletal appearance matching her name perfectly.

"Yes, Miss Skelton?" Elsbeth asked, getting to her feet as she knew she was expected to, given that this was the lady in charge of the House for Girls. "What can I do for you?"

Miss Skelton, her black hair tied back into a tight bun, gave a small disparaging sniff. "What are you doing in the schoolroom, Elsbeth? The dinner gong has sounded, has it not?"

Elsbeth did not back down, nor feel ashamed of her tardiness. "I have every intention of coming to the dining hall the moment I have finished my letter," she replied, calmly. "After all, was it not you yourself who told me that I was to leave this place just as soon as I could?" She tilted her head just a little, mousey brown curls tipping across her forehead as she did so. Her hair had always been the bane of her life, for she had such tight curls that it was almost impossible to keep them neat and tidy as she was expected to do.

Miss Skelton sniffed again. "That is no excuse, Elsbeth. I expect better from you."

Elsbeth sighed inwardly, aware that Miss Skelton was almost always disappointed with her. Ever since she could remember, Miss Skelton had been a tall, imposing figure that gave her nothing but disparaging and cutting remarks, designed to bring down her confidence. Elsbeth had, in fact, learned how to stand against Miss Skelton's venomous words, shutting down her emotions and closeting away her heart whenever the lady spoke.

"May I ask what letter it is you are writing?" Miss Skelton asked, her hands now clasped in front of her. Her long, grey dress with its high collar that hid most of her neck hung on her like a shroud, giving her an almost death-like appearance that Elsbeth hated so much.

"I have been responding to advertisements regarding governesses," Elsbeth replied, with a slight lift of her chin. "Mrs. Banks has encouraged me in this and I intend to find a position very soon. I do hope that you will give me the references I require." She lifted one eyebrow, a slight challenge in her voice as she waited for Miss Skelton to reply. Mrs. Banks, the lady who taught the girls everything from elocution to grammar, had encouraged Elsbeth in her hopes of making a life for herself outside of the Smithfield House for Girls. Mrs. Banks told her that she had all the knowledge and ability required to become a governess. In a recent spat with Miss Skelton, Elsbeth had been urged to leave the House for Girls as soon as she was able. Miss Skelton pointed out how frustrated she was that she could not throw Elsbeth out on her ear; the two things had come together to encourage Elsbeth to indeed depart. What she required of Miss Skelton was a reference to whichever one of her potential employers wrote back to her with further enquiry.

"I suppose I must," Miss Skelton replied, her voice thin. "If it means that I can get you out of this place, then I will do all I can to help you."

Elsbeth found herself smiling, feeling as though she had won victory. "Thank you, Miss Skelton. It is much appreciated, I am sure." Turning her back on the lady, she sat down again and continued to compose her letter, hearing Miss Skelton's mutter of frustration before she left the room.

Breathing a small sigh of relief, Elsbeth let her pen drift over the page, writing the same words she had written on three other occasions. Her desire to become a governess was growing with every day that she had to spend here. Even though it was the only home she had ever known, it was slowly beginning to suffocate her.

The Smithfield House for Girls was right next to the bustling Smithfield Market, but was in direct contrast to the happiness and warmth that came from there. Elsbeth often spent time looking out of her window to the market place, finding her heart filled with both happiness and pain, wishing that she could have the same joys that was in the faces of so many of those who came to the market.

They laughed and smiled more than anyone ever did in the House for Girls, mostly due to the fact that Miss Skelton was neither happy nor joyful.

Lost in thought for a moment, Elsbeth looked up from her page and let her gaze drift towards the window. Whilst her life had not been altogether bad thus far, the question about where she had come from and why she was here had always dogged her mind. Miss Skelton had never said a word, other than to state that her living allowances had been paid for – and continued to be paid for – year after year. That was why she could never throw Elsbeth out onto the street, since money was sent specifically for Elsbeth's upkeep. Elsbeth could still remember the day she had asked Miss Skelton who sent the money, only for the door to be shut in her face. That had been the day she had begun to dislike Miss Skelton intensely. Elsbeth was frustrated that the woman would not give her any information despite seeing the it upset her to have no knowledge of her birth.

Elsbeth had quietly resigned herself to the fact that she would never know, not unless her father or mother came looking for her. It was an agony that would never fully disappear from her heart, the pain of not understanding why she had been sent here as a baby. Why had her parents had turned her over to Miss Skelton instead of keeping her to raise themselves? She did not understand why Miss Skelton would not speak to her about the matter, did not understand why she would not even explain why she would not do so. That, however, was a burden Elsbeth knew she simply had to bear. Miss Skelton was not about to change her mind, in the same way that she was not about to become a warm and kind-hearted lady who cared about the charges in the House she ran.

That being said, Elsbeth knew that most of the girls here were from noblemen or gentlemen who had chosen to have a tryst outside of wedlock or outside their marriages. It was more than obvious that this was the case, for the girls were trained in all manner of gentle arts, instead of simply being fed and given a place to sleep as they would have done in the poorhouse. There were standards here, standards that both she and the others were expected to meet. Most of them might never know their fathers nor their mothers, but at least their chance at a decent life was much greater than if they'd been left at the poorhouse. There were varying choices for them in their futures – although most would become governesses or teachers in places such as these. Some would become seamstresses, others perhaps marry. Elsbeth winced as she recalled that the annual ball was due to take place in two days' time – a chance for the girls who were out to take part in a small gathering where gentlemen in the lower classes could attend in case they were in need of a wife.... or, perhaps, a mistress. She was revolted at the thought, her eyes closing tightly as she fought against the urge to run away from it all. Being now of age, she had no other choice but to attend, even though she was already responding to advertisements for governesses. Whilst Miss Skelton wanted to be rid of her, Elsbeth knew that it would be in any way she could, which included the ball and a potential husband.

Not that the gentlemen who attended were in any

way nobility. They were mostly baronets, knights, and the like, who were looking for a wife who could fulfill all their requirements whilst still being of decent standing. In addition, Elsbeth knew that many of the girls had a large dowry set aside for them, although none knew from where it had come. That was what brought such gentlemen to the ball, for even though there might be some murmuring over marriages to girls from the Smithfield House for Girls, a gentleman could overlook it should there be a large enough dowry.

Elsbeth had not thought to ask about herself, and was, therefore, quite unaware of any dowry she might have. Perhaps there would be a way for her to hide from most of the gentlemen on the evening of the ball, regardless of whether she had a dowry or not. She did not wish to marry. She wanted to experience life outside of this place, a life where she could earn her own living and make her own way if she chose. Marriage was just another four walls around her, keeping her in line.

Sighing heavily, Elsbeth finished writing her letter, sanded it carefully and then folded it up, ready to be posted.

"Please," she whispered, holding the letter carefully in her hand. "Please, let this be the way out of here. Let me find a new life, far away from Smithfield, London and Miss Skelton. Please." Closing her eyes tightly, she sent her prayer heavenwards before rising from her chair and making her way to the dining room. All she could do now was wait.

CHAPTER ONE

The following afternoon found Elsbeth finishing her embroidery piece, feeling rather pleased with herself. Embroidery had not come naturally to her and yet here she was, finishing off her final piece.

"Wonderful, Elsbeth!" Mrs. Banks exclaimed, coming to sit by her. "You should be very pleased with your work."

"Thank you, Mrs. Banks," Elsbeth replied, with a chuckle. "Although I will say that I do not understand how anyone can find any kind of enjoyment from such a thing."

Mrs. Banks smiled back, her plump face warm and friendly. "Then I should tell you that I do not particularly enjoy it myself, but it is a useful skill to have when one is seeking a husband."

Elsbeth suppressed a shudder. "Thank goodness I am not doing so."

Mrs. Banks nodded slowly. "The ball is tomorrow night. Did Miss Skelton speak to you about it?"

A niggle of worry tugged at Elsbeth's mind. "No, she did not. Why?"

For a moment, Mrs. Banks looked away, her lips thinning and Elsbeth felt herself grow tense.

"You have a large dowry, Elsbeth. I am surprised Miss Skelton has not spoken to you about this before now."

Elsbeth shook her head, firmly. "I do not care. I will not marry."

"I know, I know," Mrs. Banks said softly, putting one gentle hand on Elsbeth's. "But Miss Skelton will be sharing that news with whichever gentlemen show an interest in you at the ball. You must be prepared for that."

Elsbeth felt ice grip her heart, making her skin prickle. "I do not want to marry," she whispered, her embroidery now sitting uselessly on her lap, completely forgotten. "I know Miss Skelton wishes to get rid of me, but I cannot bring myself to preen in front of eligible gentlemen in the hope of matrimony! I want a life for myself."

Mrs. Banks gave her a small reassuring smile, one hand reaching out to rest on her shoulder. "And I am sure you will receive a return to your letters very soon," she replied, calmly, "but you must be aware of what Miss Skelton intends to do. Your dowry is very large, Elsbeth. You have clearly come from a wealthy family."

Putting her head in her hands, Elsbeth battled frustration. So much money, just out of reach. With it, she could do whatever she pleased, set up a life for herself wherever she wanted.

"Although...."

Her head jerked up as she saw Mrs. Banks look from one place to the next, her eyes a little concerned.

"Although?" Elsbeth repeated, encouraging the lady. "Although what, Mrs. Banks?"

Mrs. Banks paused for a moment before shaking her head. "Never mind. It is not something I should say."

Knowing that Mrs. Banks was the closest thing she had to a friend, Elsbeth reached across and took her hand. "Please, Mrs. Banks, tell me whatever it was you were going to say. I feel so lost already. Anything you can tell me will help." Her blue eyes searched Mrs. Banks' face, desperate to know what the lady was holding back.

"I should not be telling you this, Elsbeth," Mrs. Banks replied quietly, "but I have seen how miserable you are here and how Miss Skelton treats you. I am sorry for that. You are a free spirit and she, being as tight-laced as she is, does not understand that. She has never wanted to nurture you, she has simply wanted to contain you, and I cannot hold with that."

A lump in her throat, Elsbeth squeezed Mrs. Banks' hand. "I know," she replied, quietly. "I have valued your teaching and your friendship over the years."

Mrs. Banks drew in a long breath, her shoulders settling as she came to a decision. "As have I," she said, with a great deal more firmness. "Then I shall tell you the truth about your dowry. If you do not marry before you are twenty-one years of age, then the dowry, in all its entirety, goes to you."

Elsbeth gaped at her, her world slowly beginning to spin around her.

"Just think of it, Elsbeth," Mrs. Banks continued

softly, her voice warm. "You need only be a governess for three or four years before you will be truly free. If you are careful, I believe you will have enough to live on for the rest of your days."

Elsbeth could not breathe, her chest constricting. She could hardly believe it, could hardly take it all in, and yet she knew that what Mrs. Banks was saying was the truth. She would not lie to her.

"Why has Miss Skelton never spoken to me about this?" she asked hoarsely, as Mrs. Banks squeezed her hand. "I could have stayed here until...."

"You have answered your own question," Mrs. Banks replied, sadly. "Miss Skelton wants you gone from her establishment and she thought that, in telling you the truth, you would be filled with the urge to remain. There will be funds aplenty until you reach the age of twenty-one, for I am certain that Miss Skelton told me that whoever it is that pays for your board here would do so until either you are wed, or you are twenty-one."

Elsbeth shook her head, fervently. "That cannot be the case. Miss Skelton told me that I must find a place soon as the money that pays for me will soon cease."

"Another lie, I'm afraid," Mrs. Banks said softly, as Elsbeth felt her heart break all over again. "For whatever reason, Miss Skelton is desperate to have you gone from this place. She forbade me to speak of it to you but I knew I could not keep the truth from you. It is too great a truth to have hidden away. It would have been wrong of me to keep it to myself."

Elsbeth drew in breath after breath, her mind whirling as she tried her best to think calmly and clearly about all that had been revealed to her. Miss Skelton had always disliked her but to hide such an enormous truth from her cut Elsbeth to the bone.

"You will have your freedom one day soon," Mrs. Banks promised, putting her arm around her as Elsbeth leaned into her shoulder, just as she might have done with her mother. "Just a few more years."

Trying not to cry, Elsbeth buried her face into Mrs. Banks shoulder. "I do not think I can endure any more time here."

"Then be a governess," Mrs. Banks replied, with a small shrug. "Do whatever you wish, whatever you can until you reach twenty-one. And do not marry a gentleman, whatever you do. I know Miss Skelton is hopeful, but I would encourage you to find a way not to attend the ball tomorrow evening or, at the very least, make yourself as inconspicuous as possible."

Caught by a sudden thought, Elsbeth lifted her head. "You will not get yourself into trouble with Miss Skelton over this? I would hate for you to lose your position."

Mrs. Banks smiled softly, patting Elsbeth's cheek. "You are so caring, my dear. And no, so long as you do not reveal it to her then I think all will be well. Besides which, I do not think that Miss Skelton would dare fire me from this position – for who would she find to replace me? Her reputation as a hard woman, with little care or consideration for anyone but herself is well known." She tipped her head, her eyes alive with mirth. "Do you truly think that she would be able to find another worker with any kind of ease?"

Elsbeth had to laugh, despite her confusion and astonishment. "No, I do not think she would."

"Then you need not worry," Mrs. Banks replied, with a broad smile. "Now, off with you. Go and see if there are any letters that need to be posted so that you might take a turn about the London streets. It might help you think a little more clearly."

"I am rather overwhelmed," Elsbeth admitted, shaking her head. "Thank you for telling me so much, Mrs. Banks. I am indebted to you."

Mrs. Banks smiled again, her eyes suddenly filling with tears. "I shall miss you, when it comes time for you to leave, Elsbeth," she said quietly. "You will promise to write to me, whatever happens?"

Bending down to kiss Mrs. Banks' cheeks, Elsbeth pressed her hands for a moment. "Of course I will, Mrs. Banks. You have made my life so much better here and I will always be grateful for your love and your care for me. Thank you."

CHAPTER TWO

Whilst there were no letters to be sent, there was, according to the housekeeper who did the bidding of Miss Skelton, a need for Elsbeth to adorn the front of the House for Girls with flowers. Apparently, it was a reminder to all the gentlemen who had been invited that the ball was to happen tomorrow evening. Elsbeth did not quite understand given that so many of them had already sent their replies to confirm that, yes, they were to attend tomorrow evening's festivities.

Regardless, Elsbeth did as the housekeeper directed without making even a murmur of protest, thinking that to be outside instead of kept within the House would possibly give her the time she needed to think about all that Mrs. Banks had said. She was in no doubt that Miss Skelton had not said as much to her as regards her dowry and the wonderful age of twenty-one when she would attain her freedom, simply because she did not want Elsbeth to remain in the House for Girls. There had always been something about Elsbeth that Miss Skelton disliked, and now she was making it even more apparent that she did not care for her in the slightest. Whilst Elsbeth knew that she was, as Mrs. Banks had said, a free spirit flying in the face of Miss Skelton's harsh and firmly aligned ways, there had never been any other explanation as to why the lady had taken such a dislike to her. From her earliest memories, Elsbeth could recall Miss Skelton being dismissive and disinterested in her whilst being a *little* more jovial to the other girls. That had only bred anger and resentment in Elsbeth, who had grown more than a little frustrated with the lady's continued dislike of her; so, in her own way, she had done all she could to battle against the lady's hostility, to the point that she knew exactly what to say and do to bring her the most frustration.

Perhaps it was a little childish, Elsbeth reflected, as she picked up the basket which held the brightly colored flowers and the string with which she could tie bunches to the railings that surrounded the House for Girls. Then again, she had been a child for a very long time and only in the last few years had begun the journey towards adulthood. Miss Skelton had never changed, and Elsbeth had felt herself shrinking away from her more and more. She often sought the friendship and understanding of Mrs. Banks, a mother figure to all the orphan girls, and did not think she would have survived life here without her.

But now she had to consider what path to take. She *could* remain here until she was twenty-one, in order to come into her fortune, but that would mean over three years of Miss Skelton's dark looks and embittered words. To continue her quest to become a governess seemed the most likely path to take, for then she could simply give up that life when the time came. What would she do then? Where would she go? It was all so unexpected and yet Elsbeth was filled with a delicious excitement. To finally be free, to finally be able to build her own life....it was so near and yet so very far away.

Walking outside, Elsbeth paused for a moment as she took in the bustling market, the laughter and conversations washing over her like a wave of warmth. It was something she longed for but could never have within the House for Girls. Miss Skelton did not even like them to be near to the market, as though afraid they would smile too much for her liking.

Sighing, Elsbeth turned her back to the busy Smithfield Market and focused on her task, hoping she might be able to linger for a little while after she'd finished her task.

"Are you selling these?"

Jerked from her thoughts, Elsbeth turned to see a young man standing a short distance away from her, his eyes bright and a lazy smile on his face. Schooling her features into one of nothing more than general amiableness, she shook her head.

"No, I'm afraid not, sir. I am to place these around the railings." She did not say why, not wanting to encourage the young man to come to the Smithfield House for the ball, not when he clearly knew this was where she was from.

"I see." He moved closer to her, his smile still

lingering – and Elsbeth felt herself shrink back within herself. He was clearly something of a rake, for with his fine cut of clothes and his highly polished boots, there was no doubt that he was a gentleman – and gentlemen, from what she knew, often thought they could get whatever they wished.

He was still watching her intently, his dark brown eyes warm as they lingered on her. His dark hair was swept back, revealing his strong jaw. With his strong back and broad shoulders, Elsbeth was sure that he sent many young ladies hearts beating wildly with hopes of passion, but she had never felt more intimidated.

"Do excuse me," she murmured, making to turn away from him but only for him to catch her elbow.

"Do let me buy one from you," he said, his breath brushing across her cheek. "To remember you by, my fair flower."

Elsbeth felt a curl of fear in her stomach but chose to stand tall, her chin lifted. "No, I thank you, but I cannot sell one to you. I have a job to do. Do excuse me."

She wrenched her elbow from his hand and turned away again, telling herself to remain strong in the face of his oozing self-importance. She did not like him at all, despite his handsome features, for it was clear that he expected a simple compliment to overwhelm her to the point that she would do just as he wished.

"Well, if you will not sell one to me then perhaps you might converse with me for a time," the gentleman continued, his smile a little faded from his expression. "I am greatly inclined to know who you are."

. . .

Who is this guy? Find out in the rest of the story in the Kindle Store

MY DEAR READER

Thank you for reading and supporting my books! I hope this story brought you some escape from the real world into the always captivating Regency world. A good story, especially one with a happy ending, just brightens your day and makes you feel good! If you enjoyed the book, would you leave a review on Amazon? Reviews are always appreciated.

Below is a complete list of all my books! Why not click and see if one of them can keep you entertained for a few hours?

The Duke's Daughters Series
The Duke's Daughters: A Sweet Regency Romance
Boxset
A Rogue for a Lady
My Restless Earl
Rescued by an Earl
In the Arms of an Earl
The Reluctant Marquess (Prequel)

A Smithfield Market Regency Romance
The Smithfield Market Romances: A Sweet Regency
Romance Boxset
The Rogue's Flower

Saved by the Scoundrel
Mending the Duke
The Baron's Malady

The Returned Lords of Grosvenor Square
The Returned Lords of Grosvenor Square: A Regency
Romance Boxset
The Waiting Bride
The Long Return
The Duke's Saving Grace
A New Home for the Duke

The Spinsters Guild
A New Beginning
The Disgraced Bride
A Gentleman's Revenge
A Foolish Wager
A Lord Undone

Convenient Arrangements
A Broken Betrothal
In Search of Love
Wed in Disgrace
Betrayal and Lies
A Past to Forget
Engaged to a Friend

Landon House
Mistaken for a Rake
A Selfish Heart
A Love Unbroken

A Christmas Match
A Most Suitable Bride
An Expectation of Love

Christmas Stories
Love and Christmas Wishes: Three Regency Romance
Novellas
A Family for Christmas
Mistletoe Magic: A Regency Romance
Home for Christmas Series Page

Happy Reading!
All my love,
Rose

JOIN MY MAILING LIST

Sign up for my newsletter to stay up to date on new releases, contests, giveaways, freebies, and deals!

Free book with signup!

Monthly Facebook Giveaways! Books and Amazon gift cards!
Join me on Facebook: https://www. facebook.com/rosepearsonauthor

Website: www.RosePearsonAuthor.com

Follow me on Goodreads: Author Page

You can also follow me on Bookbub!
Click on the picture below – see the Follow button?

Printed in Great Britain
by Amazon

34433597R00143